Somebody's
Horse

Somebody's Horse

◆◆

Dorothy Nafus Morrison

Troll Associates

A TROLL BOOK, published by Troll Associates,
Mahwah, NJ 07430

Published by arrangement with Atheneum Publishers, a subsidiary
of Macmillan, Inc. For information address Atheneum Publishers,
Macmillan, Inc., 866 Third Avenue, New York, New York 10022.

First Troll Printing, 1987

Printed in the United States of America

10 9 8 7 6 5 4 3 2 1

ISBN 0-8167-1046-5

To John Daniel and Scott

Contents

++

Somebody's Horse

1

✦✦

What's Up?

Talk to your horse. Even though it cannot understand many words, it likes the sound of your voice.

YOU AND YOUR EQUINE FRIEND, page 143.

Jenny Alexander was munching an apple as she started down the carpeted hall of the bedroom wing. It was a breezy Saturday in May—Freedom Day—in the small coastal town of southern California where she lived, and all her weekend jobs were done. Now at last she could get her boots and hat, take the apple core to Cinnabar, and coax Alec to let her lead him somewhere or brush out his tail. She could almost see him already, watching over the top board of his stall. He was so special!

However, as she passed the open door of her parents' room, she heard her own name and stopped. "Jenny will never forgive us!"

Never forgive them? "Mom? What is it?" Jenny demanded.

Her mother shook her head. She had tucked the telephone under her chin and was painting her fingernails while she talked. "Korea—a remote area," she continued. "To set up a new plant. And Win . . ."— that was Jenny's father, Winthrop—"Win says he simply can't face it alone. He's only been back a few weeks."

Korea? Were her parents taking off *again*? Leaving her with fussy old Mrs. Baylor, who was always telling her to put on a sweater and for-goodness-sakes-be-careful? Yuk! Jenny slipped into the bedroom and dropped down on the carpeted floor. She could visit Cinnabar later on.

Her mother was still talking. "Yes, Auntie. I realize that."

Aunt Evelyn—of course! Mom's aunt, really, the one who had brought her up. She lived in Kansas City in a musty, dark house full of dingy cabinets and chairs that broke if you sat down too hard. The Castle of Gloom.

"What's happened?" Jenny whispered, but her mother only shook her head again.

"I'm sure that's true," she said. "A dull summer for Jenny."

Dull? Well, I guess! thought Jenny, wrapping her arms around her knees. Stuck with pokey Mrs. Baylor and her knitting and juicy cough. Mrs. Baylor would worry about Cinnabar, too.

Jenny had taken many lessons at the nearby Dexter Riding Academy on gentle, plodding Melody, of the strawberry roan coat. But for a whole year she had saved her Christmas money . . . birthday money . . . baby-sitting money . . . so she could ride this summer on Cinnabar, the long-legged jumper that all the kids adored. She had it all worked out. Alec, the instructor, had agreed and even her parents—now that she was thirteen—and it would be glorious. Only of course Mrs. Baylor might not see it that way.

"Jumping!" she might already have said in her raisin voice. "Not while *I'm* responsible!"

Maybe that's what was eating Mom. "I'm stumped. Really at rope's end," she was saying in her clipped, clear manner. "It will be nearly three months, and Mrs. Baylor, poor old soul, says she isn't up to such a long stay."

Three months! "Mom?" Jenny whispered. "Do you *have* to go?"

Her mother frowned, and now Jenny could hear Aunt Evelyn, almost loud enough to understand. Twice her mother tried to interrupt, but it was like stopping a volcano, until at last the voice ran down. "True," her mother said then. "But I can't seem to find a better plan. I don't know what we'd do, if you couldn't keep her."

Keep her! *Keep her!* Jenny sat bolt upright, feeling as if she'd been smacked in the face. So *that's* what she would never forgive! They were sending her to Aunt Evelyn's dingy old house for practically the whole summer! No kids! No horses! Nothing! She scrambled to her feet and shouted, "No!"

Her mother put her hand over the telephone mouthpiece. "*Jennifer*! I'm *talking!*" she said in a no-nonsense whisper.

"But it's about me!"

"Yes, Aunt Evelyn. I think so too." That was into the phone, and then, half under her breath, with the mouthpiece covered, "I'll explain. Later."

Jenny planted her feet wide apart and clenched her fists. She wouldn't go! Nothing would make her. She would *positively not* face a whole summer of meals in that stuffy dining room, with Aunt Evelyn and Uncle Pete droning on and on. "Mom!" she shouted again. "I'm *not going!*"

"Wait in your room," her mother whispered, with a look that meant business. "I'll see you in a minute."

"You can't make me," Jenny muttered under her breath and bolted through the door. At least the talk was winding down, with the usual promises to call again soon, and give our love to Uncle Pete, and how were Lorelei and those darling children? Lorelei was Aunt Evelyn's daughter, the one whose husband got killed.

Jenny stalked down the hall to her own pink and white room, with models of horses on every shelf. *Why* did she have a father whose company kept sending him all over the world! And a mother who thought she had to go along! *Why* couldn't she have just a plain family, like everybody else!

Throwing herself onto the bed, she picked up the sketch pad and pencil that always lay on the night stand. She wouldn't go *anywhere* for practically the whole summer. She guessed she had *something* to say about her own life! She folded back the scribbled top sheet so quickly that it tore and began to sketch a horse, a big, strong jumper, rearing and baring its teeth. That was the way she felt right then.

In a few minutes her mother appeared in the doorway. "Jenny, I'd like to talk with you."

"Okay." Jenny braced herself for a lecture on Courtesy and Being a Lady.

However, her mother only sighed and dropped into a chair, while Jenny watched from under her eyebrows. Everybody said they looked alike—tall and slender, with heavy, straight hair that was almost blond but not quite and eyes of the changeable gray-green-brown called hazel. But Jenny was sure she'd never be as cool and unruffled as her mother. Except now—for once her unflappable mom was at a loss for words.

She looked uncomfortable, too, perched on the edge of her chair. "Jenny . . ." she said.

Jenny began to draw again. "I'm not going to Aunt Evelyn's."

"Jenny . . ." Her mother drew a deep breath. "Try to understand. Your father's firm is sending him to start this new plant, and he needs me with him. I *did* stay with you last winter when he went to Taiwan. . . ."

"*So* kind of you! Really generous!" Jenny said gritting her teeth, but under her breath so her mother couldn't hear.

"What was that? Jenny—answer me."

"Nothing."

Her mother sighed again. "He's been back such a little while, and these remote assignments are lonely. You know that."

Jenny gripped the pencil more tightly. "Mom, did you forget . . . I'm going to jump on Cinnabar?"

"No, Jenny. I know how you feel. But Mrs. Baylor can't come, and I've tried everywhere—I've really tried—without any luck. So it looks as if—"

The point of Jenny's pencil broke. "It's my own money!" she said. "And you promised!"

"That's right. I didn't dream this would come up. But your father and I have considered it from every possible angle." Even though her mother didn't raise her voice—she never did—Jenny could tell she had made up her mind and wouldn't budge. "I'm sorry you overheard it like this because we were going to tell you, both of us together, this evening." A long pause, then she continued more crisply. "In any case, it can't be helped, so we'll all have to make the best of it. Three months isn't forever, and you can ride Cinnabar in the fall."

Jenny stared out the window at the bougainvillea, scarlet against the fence, with palm trees waving just beyond. How could it be such a nice, sunny day, when this—this *awful thing*—was happening! The cruel, hot Santa Anna wind ought to be blowing, or something.

Her mother reached for her hand, but Jenny jerked it away. "I haven't given up—quite," her mother said. "There are two weeks before we go, and we'll keep looking. A summer camp?"

"Ugh!" Jenny had tried a camp once, and once was enough.

"Jenny . . . it's really very kind of Aunt Evelyn to take care of you, and I expect you to cooperate."

No answer.

"It's not the end of the world."

"I won't do it."

"Jenny—listen to me. Your father has no choice, and I'm going with him this time. Nothing you say will change that. So you might as well face it and stop wallowing in gloom. And for goodness sakes, *please* don't take off on one of your harebrained projects. Aunt Evelyn understands how disappointed you are. She'll make it up to you."

"She can't. Nobody could." Picking up another pencil, Jenny shaded in the horse's tail.

"We'll arrange the lessons in the fall. Lots of lessons. More than you could possibly pay for with your own money."

Bribery! It won't work! thought Jenny. Mom doesn't care. But at once she realized that wasn't quite fair. Mom was in a spot, too. Dad needed her in Korea, just as much as she, Jenny, needed her at home, and she couldn't be in both places at once. Only . . .

Aunt Evelyn! "I'm not going," she said again in a strangled voice, and began to sketch the horse's mane. After a moment her mother stood up and went away.

That evening, right after dinner, Jenny walked through the soft California twilight to the riding academy, where the attendant knew her and allowed her to enter the barn. She strolled down the springy board floor, listening to the stamp of heavy feet, the snuffles and occasional soft whinnies. A few flies were circling, pigeons on the rafters were cooing, and golden, dusty sunlight slanted in through the wide door. The air was warm, scented with hay and disinfectant and horse. Heaven, Jenny thought.

And here was Cinnabar's stall, his long, red-brown face looking at her over the top board. "Cinnabar, we've got trouble," she told him. "My mom says I can't ride you this summer, after all. That I won't even *be* here. But I'm not giving up. I'll stay if I possibly can. And if I do have to go, I've saved a lot of money, so I can learn to jump with you in the fall."

She held out her hand for him to nuzzle into it with his velvety nose. "You're the most wonderful horse in the whole world." She stroked his bony forehead, bristly going up and smooth going down, and rubbed his head just behind the ears, which made him shut his eyes and hold very still. She stayed there a long time, talking softly, then turned and started home.

A week later and twelve hundred miles away, in the small town of Pine Valley, Wyoming, seven-year-old Lissie Burnett flung open the door and charged into the house, closely followed by Chip, who was five. "Mommie!" Lissie called. "You'll never guess what . . ."

Just behind her, Chip shrieked. "There's a . . ."

"*Shut—the—door!*" At the sound of their mother's voice, Lissie obediently backtracked, bumping into Chip.

Closing the outside door with a bang, she pounded up the narrow stairs, which were steep and walled in, like a box. "Mommie!" she shouted again. "We've got a *horse!*"

"It's in our *barn!*" Chip's shrill voice shrieked on the last word.

"Mr. Brown gave it to us," Lissie gasped. The Browns had just moved out of the rambling old house that the children's mother, Lorelei, had recently bought. "It's a great big one. Right there in the stall."

Lorelei was in an upstairs bedroom, gingerly surveying a heap of dirty rags. "And I've a pet crocodile in my bathtub," she said, without turning around. She'd have to get a truck to carry away all the junk —old clothes, newspapers, broken furniture, garbage. What was it her grandad used to say? *Tarnation!* Tarnation again, and Triple Tarnation! She'd been crazy to think she could buy a house and move into it, all by herself, even if it was a bargain.

Lissie plucked at her elbow. "Honest! It's a real horse. Just standing there. It isn't even *moving!*"

"Except its tail," Chip added. "It swishes."

"And it stomped once," Lissie conceded. "Why did Mr. Brown give us their horse?"

"Lissie—Chip." Lorelei sighed. The Browns had finally left, not fifteen minutes ago, right after she had come to check out the place and see what had to be done. She'd heard Mr. Brown's voice outside, talking to the children, and then the rattle of his ancient car going down the lane. "I've got too much on my mind to play games. Some other time."

"But it's true!" Lissie insisted, blue eyes wide. "Mr. Brown said he had a s'prise for us. He said it was all ours. And he told us to go look in the barn. And . . ."

". . . and we *did*!" Chip was jumping up and down. "And it's a *horse*! It's our *very own*! He *gave* it to us. And some hay, too."

"He said he'd been waiting around all morning for us to show up so he could tell us about it," Lissie added.

Lorelei shook her head. "They're scatty people," she said. "I grant you that. But nobody's that scatty. Try again, you two. You almost had me scared."

Drawing down the corners of her mouth, Lissie assumed her most dignified manner. "Mr. Brown said we could take it to the dog-food place if we don't want it." And then, discarding dignity, "But of course we wouldn't do that . . . would we, Mommie?"

"*Please!*" Chip's eyes filled with tears.

"A horse . . . An abandoned horse . . . Nobody's

horse . . . Or . . . Somebody's horse . . ." Lorelei's eyes took on their most far-away look. "Real-l-ly!"

"You could put it in a book!" Lissie exclaimed. Lorelei wrote mysteries, at night when the children were in bed. Maybe she'd write the next one about a horse. An abandoned horse. A left-behind horse.

But Lissie was tugging at her arm. "Mommie, what are we going to do about it?" she asked.

"Do . . . ? Well . . ." Lorelei came back to the here-and-now. "Write to the Browns, I suppose. Find out why they dumped it. Get rid of it, one way or another. We surely haven't time to take care of any more critters than we've already acquired." Smiling, she touseled Chip's hair. "You included."

"I could take care of it," Chip asserted. "Me and Lissie could together. A horse would be neat-oh."

"You've plenty of pets without that." Lorelei put her hands on her hips and once more surveyed the incredible mess. "Right now, you've a whole roomful of stuff to pack up—all that *good junk* you wouldn't let me get rid of. So let's go home and get busy, and I'll have a truck in here Monday to clear this place out. Also a crew to de-louse it." She added with a giggle, "Don't look so lugubrious. Do you realize that we're householders at last? With a leaky roof, plumbing that gurgles, a basement full of empty whiskey bottles. And now—unless it's another of your so-called jokes—somebody's horse." She turned around, wiping her hands on the plaid shirttail that dangled over her jeans. "You still maintain it's really and truly there?"

Lissie and Chip solemnly nodded.

"All right—show me," Lorelei said and followed them down the stairs.

2

++

The Horse
Nobody Wanted

*Try not to expect too much. Your horse
wants to please you, but may not be able to
measure up.*

YOU AND YOUR EQUINE FRIEND, page 128.

"We are now beginning our descent to Rock
Springs." The steward's voice rasped over the loud-
speaker. "Will all passengers please check to make
sure their seatbelts are securely fastened."

Almost there! thought Jenny, as she checked the
strap. It had been a long day.

Early that morning her parents had put her on the
plane, with a whole blizzard of directions: *Don't take
any chances.* That was her dad, tall and slim in his
business suit, grinning down at her, but with a hint
of worry in his eyes. *Horseflesh can be treacherous,
especially a range animal, maybe half trained. And
you're not exactly noted for prudence.*

15

Her mother had been worried too, but for a different reason. *Help Lorelei as much as you can*, she'd said about a hundred times. *She has two small children, plus a job*. She'd added a whole lot about arrangements and remember-this-is-your-choice and be-sure-to-write-every-week. Routine stuff.

Mom had been trying, really trying, but even while she ladled out good advice as if it were chicken soup, her eyes were far off, and Jenny could tell that on the inside she was thinking, what would the weather be like in Korea, and did she remember to pack her address book? Jenny's mind had been on other things, too. Such as, what kind of horse would it be? And—scary thought—could she take care of it all by herself?

Well, she'd soon find out. She eagerly pressed her forehead against the tiny window and she caught her breath. If it were California, she'd be looking at the ocean, with a blue and white line of surf and clusters of friendly red roofs. But here everything was so big! So empty! Hardly any roads. No towns. Just an enormous tumble of dark hills, with great sweeping green valleys between and snow-capped mountains around the edge.

For a moment she had a crazy desire to turn around and go home. "Take me back!" she wanted to cry out. "This is a terrible idea!" But of course she couldn't do that. By tomorrow her parents would be on their way to Korea, leaving her to spend the summer with a family of cousins she hardly knew. And a strange horse was waiting for her—a horse that nobody wanted.

She had been thinking about it all the way, first on the huge jet from San Diego to Salt Lake City, then on this smaller one. Thanks to Aunt Evelyn, the plans had been made so fast that Jenny still felt dizzy.

First had come an exuberant phone call from Kansas City. "I have an idea. Much better for Jenny than putting up with Peter and me. Now don't say no until you hear all about it," Aunt Evelyn had insisted, while, at her mother's nod, Jenny listened on the extension telephone.

"It's a horse," Aunt Evelyn continued. "I told you Lorelei had bought a few acres of ground and a dilapidated old house. All she could afford in that booming tourist town. Well, the most astonishing thing has happened. Really, it almost seems as if it were *meant*. The people who had been renting the house have simply moved out and left a horse in the barn."

"Left a *horse*!" Jenny's mother exclaimed. "Surely not!"

"Surely yes. Horse. H-O-R-S-E. Now don't ask why, because I don't know. And don't ask what kind, because a beast is a beast as far as I'm concerned. But no doubt it has four legs and eyes and ears and probably not a scrap of sense. Anyhow, it's a horse. And I know Jenny wants to spend her summer in the saddle. So—here's the way."

Jenny had met Lorelei occasionally at family gatherings. Being Aunt Evelyn's daughter, she was really Mom's cousin, but she was lots younger, and glamorous, with wavy dark hair and wide-apart blue eyes that tilted up at the corners. She had studied journalism in college, had met her husband when they were students, and they'd bought a weekly newspaper in the little town of Pine Valley, Wyoming, so he could be close to fishing and big game. After they'd put out the paper together for a few years, he had been killed in a hunting accident, leaving Lorelei to keep it going. And now Aunt Evelyn wanted Jenny to spend the summer there.

"You mean, ask Lorelei to take her?" asked Jenny's mother. "Alone as she is, and with those children? And just moved? She couldn't possibly take on an extra person, plus a horse."

"Nonsense!" Aunt Evelyn brushed aside all doubts. "I assume you'd pay her something, which will come in handy, what with a house that needs a fortune in repairs, plus two youngsters to keep in shoeleather. She'll be glad to have a few dollars coming in. Maybe Jenny could help with the children, too. You know, Lorelei is still on that paperback kick . . . as if she didn't get enough writing on the job."

Here Aunt Evelyn paused for breath, which gave Jenny's mother a chance to break in. "I never heard of such a thing! Abandoning a horse? Won't the owners come after it?"

Just about the time I get there, Jenny had thought, *and then I'll be out of luck.*

"They don't want it. Absolutely not." Aunt Evelyn's voice had been loud and assured. "Lorelei's already inquired, and these people relinquished all claim. Actually, Lorelei was going to get rid of it, but she said that if Jenny comes, she'll keep it until fall."

"Well . . ." Jennie's mother seemed only half convinced. "It sounds preposterous to me, but I'll talk it over with Win."

"Good. There's no problem, then. I was certain it would all work out." With the cheerful assurance of a job well done. Aunt Evelyn released the phone.

No problem, Jenny had thought. *Except to me, having to leave Cinnabar and all my friends and try to ride a miserable old horse that nobody wants. Still —Wyoming or Kansas City! Lorelei or Aunt Evelyn!*

"I'll take Wyoming. At least I'll have *something* to ride," she'd insisted.

"It's too much to ask of Lorelei," her mother protested.

"I won't be any trouble. I'll help her a lot. I'll baby-sit. Wash the car. Clean the house. *Honest!*"

"Aunt Evelyn and Uncle Pete said they'd take you on a little trip."

"No! I'm *not* . . . going . . . *there!*" She'd made every promise she could think of, sensible or not, plus a whole lot of threats. "I'll run away! Come back here and sleep at the Dexter!"

In the end, her mother had sighed and given in. So

here she was in the air above Wyoming, and she didn't even know whether she'd have a gelding or a mare, black, white, or gray.

With a gentle thump the plane touched ground, and soon Jenny was plodding up the ramp.

"Jenny! Jenny Alexander! Over here!"

She quickly spotted two shrieking children with short fair hair that curled at its ends and the same tip-tilted blue eyes as their mother. Lorelei stood beside them, beautiful as Jenny remembered, in a white sweater and skirt, her dark hair cut short, with thick, side-swept bangs. "Here, Jenny!" Her lips clearly formed the words, even though they were lost in the airport noise.

"Jenny! Jenny!" The children screamed again, jumping up and down, and all of a sudden Jenny was thankful Aunt Evelyn had said they had a big house. With her stomach doing loop-the-loops, she walked up the carpeted ramp, duffle bag bumping against her knees.

At the top, Lorelei wrapped her in a bear hug. "Jenny, this is my gang," she said. "As if you couldn't guess. Here's Chip—and Lissie. Have you a kiss for Cousin Jenny, you two?" The children turned suddenly shy and stared at the floor. "No? Well, at least tell her hello."

They looked up, mumbled inaudible words, and were promptly seized with the giggles, shoving each other and turning quite red.

An instant family, Jenny thought, as they started

toward the baggage claim section. And I've got to live with them all summer long. Talk about dumb-dumb ideas! "Do you still have the horse?" she asked. "Has the owner turned up?"

"Not yet," Lorelei replied. "And according to the Browns, nobody will."

"Is it a mare? Your mother didn't know."

"Gelding . . ." Lorelei started to reply, but Chip interrupted.

"It's a man horse. A great big one." He clamped his jaw shut again and glared at the ceiling.

A gelding. Like Cinnabar, Jenny thought, and asked, "Is it any good? Steady? Kind?"

"*I* wouldn't know. I never did ride much," Lorelei replied with a wry smile. "The kids seem to think so."

"He doesn't bite or anything. He's real friendly!" Lissie exclaimed. With this the children forgot their shyness and launched into a stream of talk about the horse, Chip's rabbits, and Lissie's cat. The chatter went on and on while they collected Jenny's suitcase, went to a fast-food stand for hamburgers all around, and piled into the car for the three-hour drive to Pine Valley.

By now it was late afternoon, and the sky began to acquire a tinge of red. The land was strange and lonesome, with long black shadows that outlined clumps of brush, gigantic gray rocks, and occasional jagged gullies. Farther away was a backdrop of hills, dark with forests, stretching on and on, misty blue against the sky.

"Range land and wilderness," Lorelei said with a dry smile. "A magnet for tourists and dudes. Too many people, the oldtimers often say. But they keep the town afloat."

As soon as the children fell asleep, Lorelei launched into the questions strangers always asked—what subject did Jenny like best, and did she go out for chorus or play volley ball or swim? Although Jenny answered politely, she felt lost and scared. It seemed as if time were standing still, as if the road and the day would run on forever, or as if she were caught on a conveyor belt, with an endless procession of hills rolling past the windows and sky the color of fire. But just at dusk they drove through the small town of Pine Valley, and at its farther edge Lorelei stopped beside a shabby house which was almost swallowed by its own wide porch.

"Here we are," she said. "We're not settled, Jenny, but such as it is, it's home sweet home." She turned around. "Wake up, you two sleepyheads."

Tumbling out of the car, they carried the suitcases into a large, old-fashioned kitchen, with wooden cupboards, a round table in the center, and a floor of gray-painted boards. In one corner was an enormous birdcage holding a huge, purple bird with yellow circles around its eyes. It stood on a perch and cocked its head from side to side.

"This is Honey—my Hyacinth Mackaw," Chip proudly said. "I named him Honey because he's so sweet. Tell Jenny hello, Honey. She's going to live with us."

Sweet? This menacing creature? Jenny thought, as he clawed his way up the bars of the cage and finally said something that sounded like "Ah-oh."

"See! Isn't that neat!" Chip exclaimed. "I'm teaching him to sing too. But he won't do it yet for strangers."

"He's handsome, all right" Jenny agreed. "Is he as fierce as he looks?"

"He isn't fierce at all. He likes me," Chip replied, putting his finger through the wires. "Nice Honey! Pretty bird." When Honey snapped at the finger, Chip jerked it back. "Hey!"

Lorelei smiled and touseled his hair. "A present from my mother. Chip was so crazy about birds that she said, 'He wants a bird—he'll have a bird.' And next time she came to visit, here was Honey."

Aunt Evelyn? A softy? Jenny blinked in surprise.

Lissie now reached for her hand. "We've got a *stairway*," she proudly asserted, dragging her toward a narrow door in the kitchen wall. "Your room's up here, and so are mine and Chip's. But Mommie sleeps downstairs."

They labored up the boxed-in staircase, with Chip and Lissie tugging at the duffle-bag, while Jenny carried the suitcase. Unopened packing boxes lined the hall, at the end of which was her room, small, with thick blankets on the narrow bed, and flowered wallpaper curling at the seams. The floor humped up in the middle, and the uncurtained windows had dark green pull-down shades.

"That's because of the sun," Lissie importantly explained. "It shines on this side in the morning."

While the children watched with unblinking stares, Jenny unpacked her duffle bag—riding breeches, jacket, hat, boots. She didn't suppose she'd wear them here, except the boots, but she'd been determined to bring them along. "The horse?" she asked. "Shall we go see him now?"

"Sure," agreed Chip, pulling her toward his room. "But first here's my robot." He brought out a small, stocky, creature with flashing eyes and hooks for hands. "See . . . he can pick up these boxes and he can walk. All I have to do is tell him—but I have to say it the same way every time."

He spoke into a black microphone. "Go, boy." The creature moved forward. "Stop boy." The robot continued blindly on. "Stop boy." Chip's voice became a shout. "*Stop—stop boy!*" He stuck out his chin and glared. "*Hey! Stop!*"

"Well." Chip turned off the control. "I'm still learning. But isn't he *neat!*"

"He's wonderful," Jenny said, trying to sound enthusiastic. "And now—the horse?"

"Sure. But I've got some pollywogs, too." He led her to a fishbowl of murky water in which half a dozen large tadpoles were darting back and forth.

"I used to catch pollywogs," Jenny told him.

"Honest? Did they get legs?"

"Only a few," Jenny sadly admitted. "Most of them died."

"Well, these aren't going to die. I'm going to raise them into frogs," Chip asserted. "I have some rabbits, too, but they're outside."

"That's nice. But . . . Chip? The horse?"

"Sure, in just a minute. Let's look at my train." An elaborate electric set on a plywood board was standing in the corner. Nothing would do but Jenny must sit admiringly by while he ran it forward and backward, and showed off a special car on which a tiny metal policeman chased a tiny metal tramp.

"It was my dad's when he was a kid," Chip explained. "He gave it to me before—before *that* happened."

"It's just wonderful," Jenny agreed. "I'd like it too, if I had a train like that."

Then they had to troop to Lissie's room to see her collection of stuffed animals, and pet Pinkie, the big yellow cat that was sleeping on the bed. By the time they started down the path behind the house, it was so dark they carried flashlights.

"My rabbits are right there," said Chip as they passed a large cage.

"I'd like to see them, Chip," Jenny told him, "but they're asleep now. Show them to me tomorrow."

"Okay." And at last they entered the barn.

Holding her breath, Jenny stepped to the nearest stall and turned her light on the animal that stood in it. "Oh!" Her heart sank with a thud she could almost hear. She hadn't expected much, but this. . . .

The dim light showed a gelding, head sagging, long-legged, and so thin his ribs and hip bones stuck out. His coat, which was an indefinite dark shade, was rough and caked with mud. Dirty hair dangled over his eyes, his feet were similarly fringed, his mane looked like a bird's nest. Just as Jenny entered the stall, he gave a hollow cough, then stood still, as meek and listless as if he would never willingly move again. However, when Jenny held out her hand, he lifted his head with a soft nicker.

"We were going to wash him before you came, but we didn't have time," Lissie explained.

"We had to help move," added Chip. "And—and—"

"We've been swamped," Lissie finished. "Anyway, that's what Mommie said. If you hadn't come we were prob'ly going to take him to the dog food place."

"Dog food!" Jenny was shocked. "The poor old thing!" But dog food may be all he's fit for, she thought against her will. He couldn't even hold me up.

She tried to think of something pleasant to say. "Well—I've wanted a horse to take care of, and this one needs it all right. We'd better feed him, right now. Where is his grain?"

"Grain?" Lissie sounded surprised. "All we gave him was hay. And water. And Mommie helped us clean his stall—a few times." She glanced at the stall floor.

A few times were obviously not enough, thought Jennie, but she said only, "Well—hay then, for today. Tomorrow we'll do better." She put a generous amount into the feed rack, at which the horse lowered his head and began to eat greedily, whiffling into the corners for every stray wisp. "Hungry, aren't you?" Jenny murmured, stroking the bony neck.

Even if I get him fattened up, how could I bear to ride this . . . this *thing*? she thought as they started back to the house. After planning on Cinnabar?

"What do you make of our critter?" asked Lorelei when they were back in the kitchen and Chip had closed the door with his usual bang.

"Well . . ." Again Jenny searched for some positive words. "He's thin. But he seems gentle. I think I'll like him." She tried to sound sincere, and it was true in a way. She *liked* any horse, even this one.

"We'll see," Lorelei replied with a wry smile. "I don't know anything about horses, but that poor creature looks hopeless to me. I tried to tell my mother so, but she hardly listened. I hope she didn't build him up too much."

"Oh—not at all," said Jenny, although she couldn't forget Aunt Evelyn's breezy remarks. "Do you think —has he been ridden much?"

"I've no idea," said Lorelei with a sigh. "Not by us, anyway. All I did was have some hay sent out, so he won't collapse of starvation. And Jenny—can you believe it?—the children want to turn him into a racer." She laughed, and Jenny tried to laugh, too.

"I think I'll go to bed," she said, stifling a yawn. "I've had a pretty long day."

"Of course," Lorelei agreed. "Don't worry if you hear me rattling around half the night. I'll be unpacking. And if you need anything, let me know."

Jenny's hand was on the knob of the stair door. "I'm sure I'll be all right. Good night now."

" 'Night." Lorelei hesitated. "Remember, Jenny—I'm here, if you think of anything, or even if you just want to talk."

Jenny didn't answer.

"Jenny, I hope you'll feel at home."

Although Lorelei looked as if she would like to say more, Jenny fled. She wished her cousin would just *keep quiet*, because her eyes were swimming and her mouth felt tight, and she wanted to get off by herself before she began to absolutely howl.

In her own room, blinking back tears, she opened her large suitcase and took out her latest birthday presents: a pair of curry combs, a stiff dandy-brush, a soft body brush, a comb, and a hoof pick. She'd been so thrilled when she received them—for Cinnabar, of course. And now this! Anyway, they'll come in handy, she thought, as she rubbed her thumb on the stiff bristles. She couldn't imagine a horse that needed them more.

She also took out her sketch pad and pencils, and a book, *You and Your Equine Friend*, which explained absolutely everything about taking care of a horse—except how to turn a sick, old one into something young and lively. Placing it in the top drawer of her chest, she decided to unpack the rest tomorrow, brushed her teeth, climbed into bed, and propped herself up with both pillows.

She had begun a sketch of Cinnabar clearing a jump, when she heard Lorelei climb the stairs, and giggles from the children's rooms.

"Are you okay?" Lorelei asked a few minutes later, standing in the doorway. "Find everything? I notice your light's still on."

"I'm fine. Just fine." Jenny darkened the top railing on Cinnabar's jump.

"I didn't know you were interested in drawing, Jenny. May I see?" Lorelei crossed to the bed. "Why —it's really nice."

"It's only a sketch."

"More than that. It's good." Lorelei hesitated. "Jenny . . . I know this can't be easy for you—all your summer plans knocked haywire—coming to a family you hardly know, with two little kids underfoot, and me so busy. And this place must look pretty forlorn right now, although they tell me it's a good solid house, once I get it repaired and painted."

"It's a nice house, Lorelei." Surely sometimes it was all right to fib.

"Well—given a new roof—and a paint job—and some modern plumbing and wiring, I think it has possibilities. It's one of the oldest in town." Lorelei was talking eagerly now, as if she really liked it. "I already have some antique furniture, and little by little, if I save my pennies, I'll get it fixed up." Her lips curved in a wry smile. "A five-year plan. Or more likely ten!"

Jenny began to draw again, talking as she worked. "Lorelei . . . that horse must belong to *somebody*. Do you think they'll come after him?"

Lorelei sat down beside her on the bed. "I really think that nobody in this whole world wants him. When I telephoned Mr. Brown—he's in Chicago— he said a friend left the horse with them. And when I asked about the friend, Mr. Brown just laughed— not a very nice laugh, Jenny—and said, 'That's all right, ma'am. He won't bother you none.'"

Lorelei mimicked the conversation in such a comical, nasal voice that Jenny couldn't help laughing.

"Well . . . I'll see what I can do with him." Her cousin seemed to be waiting for Jenny to say something more, but nothing she could think of was halfway sensible. *I know I'll like it here?* That wasn't true. *I'll hate it?* Insulting. She drew a few more lines.

In a moment Lorelei began to talk again, something about what her mother had said, but Jenny only half listened because things were suddenly blurred.

"I'll try," she managed.

Why didn't her cousin go away?

"Well . . ." Lorelei suddenly jumped up. "Let me know whatever you need, and I'll see you in the morning. 'Night, now."

"Good night," mumbled Jenny, and at last she was alone.

Turning to a fresh new page, she started to draw another picture of Cinnabar in a pasture, with one foot lifted and neck arched. But the tears made it hard to see well. She erased a few strokes, added some—and she had a picture of a long-legged horse with a drooping head. A horse that nobody wanted.

I don't want him either, thought Jenny, as she tore off the page and crumpled it into a ball. Snapping out the light and slipping under the heavy blankets, she buried her face in a pillow. At least keep *quiet*, she fiercely told herself. The whole family doesn't have to hear. Only—why did I come? Why didn't I know a scheme of Aunt Evelyn's would turn out like this?

Her dad always said that when life hands you a lemon, you should make lemonade. Life had handed her a lemon all right, a great big sour one, without a grain of sugar to go with it. She should have gone to Aunt Evelyn's—at least there was a swimming pool not far away.

But it was too late to even think of that. She was here, in a falling-down house with a falling-down horse, and this pokey summer was going to last for almost twelve whole weeks. That seemed like forever.

3

✦✦✦✦✦✦✦✦✦✦✦✦✦✦✦✦✦✦✦✦✦✦✦✦✦✦✦✦✦✦✦✦✦✦✦

The Wrong Way to Bathe a Horse

The horse that is well cared-for and properly groomed does not often need a complete bath.
YOU AND YOUR EQUINE FRIEND, page 61.

When Jenny awoke the next morning, she lay still for a few minutes with her eyes closed, and a vague feeling that something was wrong. Of course . . . she was in Wyoming, and it was big and bare and lonesome. She had seen the horse. And that was worse.

Lumpy as the bed was, she wanted to stay there all day with her head under the covers. But she could hear someone singing in a high, clear voice—Lorelei? And was that the smell of coffee? Everyone was stirring, so Jenny reluctantly pushed back the blankets and climbed out.

At the first touch of the floor she gasped, for she had a fuzzy carpet at home, and these bare boards were like ice. But daylight was bright through the cracks around the green shade, so she curled her toes against the cold, ran quickly to a window, and gave the shade a jerk that made it zip all the way to the top and flap around and around on its roller.

Outside, the sun was high already, shining on Chip's rabbit hutch, the faded red barn, and purple hills farther on. If only Cinnabar were waiting for her out there! She could have glorious rides away into the countryside, and she'd find some places to jump, too! But the only horse here was a worn-out old thing who looked as if every breath might be his last.

Just then a voice called, "Chip!" and he answered, "All right. Coming." I'd better hurry, Jenny thought as she hastily pulled on jeans and a blue plaid shirt, topped by a sweater. Were Wyoming mornings always so cold? Running down the narrow stairs, she entered the kitchen, where Chip was seated at the round table, with Honey cozily perched on his shoulder. Lissie was crouched in a corner, feeding Pinkie, while Lorelei stirred something at the stove.

As Jenny entered the room, Lissie began to sing at the top of her lungs. "I-I-I-'ve a little kitty at home, and she kno-o-o-ws me." Her voice was clear and true, very high and very loud.

"Pipe down, Lissie," Chip commanded. "Honey doesn't like it."

"Ah-oh!" said Honey, but the song went on.

"See! He said, stop!" Chip crossed his eyes to look at his own nose and pushed out his mouth in a round, red "O."

"Mommie!" Lissie squealed. "Chip's doing that thing with his eyes again!"

Lorelei turned around just in time to see Lissie stick out her tongue. "Hey, you two. Cool it," she commanded. "Honey doesn't like a squabble, either. And hi, Jenny. Sleep okay?"

"Like everything," Jenny answered. "I was really tired."

"We all were." Lorelei spooned oatmeal into four bowls. "Those were late hours last night, for us."

They took their places, but when Chip saw his steaming cereal, he scowled. "Oatmeal again? *Some* kids get Choco-Wheat."

"No complaints, Mr. Chip," Lorelei ordered. "You know perfectly well why we have this." She handed Jenny a pitcher. "Tomato juice? Coffee? Milk?"

"Milk will be fine," Jenny replied, filling her glass. She reached for the brown sugar. "And Chip, what's wrong with oatmeal? I really like it."

"Thanks, Jenny. I need an ally," murmured Lorelei as she dropped into a chair. She was silent for a few moments, sipping her coffee. "You're probably wondering about our routine," she continued. "Actually, it's simple. I'll take off when Mrs. Wilson comes. In winter the kids are in school, but for summer vacation she holds the fort at home while I'm working."

"She's real old," volunteered Lissie. "She reads most of the time. But she's pretty nice."

"Except she's scared of bugs," added Chip.

"She does very well," said their mother. "She has a lot to put up with, corralling you two wild Indians." A smile softened the words. "I'm back soon after five, and then it's dinner and whatever comes along—unpacking boxes, right now. And that's about it, except after they go to bed is my time to write."

"Your newspaper?"

"Well—sometimes I bring the office home. But most of my evenings are for real writing. The kids know it's what their lives are worth to bother me then, and they're pretty good about it."

"She wrote a book," Lissie said, looking up from her bowl.

"And she has to write another," Chip added, "or they'll put her in jail."

Lorelei laughed. "Not quite. I must have sounded fiercer than I intended. But I've signed a contract, so I really do have to stick with it. I set up my typewriter the day after we moved."

"It sounds like a lot of work," said Jenny, remembering the promises she'd made to her mother. *I won't be any trouble. I'll help them, a lot.* "Do you need anything? I can cook a little—and—"

"Well—we'll see. For today, you'll have your hands full getting acquainted with that pathetic creature in the barn."

Just then a knock sounded on the door, and a woman bustled in—round-faced, round-bodied, with plump arms and hands that bulged around her many rings.

"Here's Mrs. Wilson now," Lorelei said, introducing them. "If you have any problems, Jenny, she's an expert."

"We'll do fine," Mrs. Wilson said, with a ringing laugh, as she set down her bright red tote bag. "Don't you worry about a thing."

"I won't," Lorelei promised. "Even if I wanted to, I haven't a smidgeon of time once I hit the office. And now run along, all of you. Mrs. Wilson will do the washing up." She kissed the children, gathered up her briefcase and handbag, and was out the door before Jenny could catch her breath.

"So," said Mrs. Wilson, settling herself at the table with a cup of coffee. "You're the California cousin. Come to ride a horse."

"That's right. I know it sounds funny."

"Not at all. Many a girl would give her eyeteeth to do just what you're doing." Mrs. Wilson liberally sugared her coffee, then launched into a long, jolly account of girl riders she had known. She was still naming them over when Jenny finished her oatmeal and carried her dishes to the sink.

"And now I'm going to the barn. I've a horse to wash."

"Can we come?" asked Chip.

"Please?" added Lissie.

"Haven't you something else to do? Feed your rabbits? Or . . ."

"We'd rather help you." Shoving his hands into his pockets, Chip stared up at Jenny.

"Play with your friends?"

"No. The horse is more fun."

So, after all those promises, I'll have to see it through, thought Jenny. "Well, come along," she said. "But you'll find that washing a horse is a hard job."

"We don't care. Besides, he *knows* us," Lissie firmly replied.

"Let's see, now . . ." How was she going to manage with a pair of kids underfoot? "You could pull him some grass."

"He's got hay. He likes that better."

Jenny sighed. "All right, but you can't go into the stall. He might get excited and kick you." She ran upstairs for her grooming tools.

Outside, the sky was incredibly blue and a chill breeze rustled the fir and cottonwood trees. With Chip and Lissie chattering beside her, Jenny hurried down the path, past the rabbits' hutch and runway, and entered the barn. It contained only two stalls on one side of a wide aisle, feed room and tack room on the other, and its equipment consisted of a small stack of hay, a bridle hanging on a hook, a brown saddle on a shelf, and a pile of dusty blankets.

And here was the horse, almost motionless—head hanging, ears flat, dull-eyed, and coughing. However, when Jenny stepped into the stall and held out her hand, he nickered, then took a single plodding step forward to nuzzle into it. "Kind of a nice old thing, you are, even if you do dodder," she murmured, giving his nose a tickle. He took another step, laid his long head against her upper arm, and when she began to rub him between the ears, he closed his eyes with a blissful sigh.

Now, by daylight, she could see that his coat was dark brown, with an irregular white splotch on his forehead. "Really, he's sort of a pretty color," Jenny told the children, who had dragged a large box into the adjoining stall and climbed onto it to look over the top board.

"What are you going to name him?" Lissie asked.

"I haven't a clue."

"Brownie would be nice. I have a book about brownies, and he's all brown."

"Chocolate?" This was Chip. "Pumpkin Pie? Pancake? Something to eat would fit right in with Honey."

"Well . . . let's see what he looks like when he's clean," said Jenny.

"Okay. We'll call him Horse for now."

"Horse he is." Sighing, Jenny brushed back his forelock, which hung in a shaggy mat over his eyes.

"He needs a barber," Lissie said from her perch.

"He does," Jenny agreed. "But we'll wash him first, and then I'll work on the hair."

"I'll get buckets," offered Chip, and like a flash the children ran into the house, while Jenny tried to figure out how she could manage. She'd bathed Melody at the Dexter, but always with a wash rack and warm running water, and there was nothing like that here.

First she must get the animal outside and tie him up. That shouldn't be a problem because he was already wearing a halter, and a couple of ropes were hanging on a post at the head of his stall. Jenny examined them. One was short, but frayed and discolored; one was newer, but much too long. The short one would be better, she thought. The other would get in the way.

"At least you're a tractable old thing," she said, as Horse willingly let her lead him into the small, rough yard that adjoined the barn. Two stout rings were fastened to the outside wall, so Jenny tied the rope to one of those, and by then Chip and Lissie appeared with buckets, a plastic bottle of Lorelei's shampoo, and a scrubbing brush.

"We'll start by currying him," Jenny said to the eager children. "That will get rid of the mud." Taking off her heavy shirt and hanging it on the fence, she reflected that since they were determined to stay, she'd better keep them busy. "I'll use this metal curry comb. Lissie, here's a plastic one for you—rub it around in circles. And Chip, how about a brush? Go this way, the direction of the hairs. Stay up front by his shoulders, both of you."

They all began to work, with the children jabbering and Horse almost motionless, eyes closed. Now and then he heaved a tremendous sigh.

"Do you like to have us scratch your itches?" Jenny asked. "This must be your first grooming in ever so long." She worked from shoulders to hips, first one side and then the other, stopping often to scrape bunches of dead winter hair from her brush.

"A horse is *very* big!" Lissie exclaimed after a while.

"It is," Jenny agreed.

Finally she decided the animal was as clean as comb and brush could make him. "It's time now for washing," she said. "We've got to have lots of water."

"I'll get the hose!" exclaimed Chip.

"All right."

But it reached only halfway to the barn, so Jenny led Horse up the path. "We'll have to do it here," she told the children, as she tied him to a low-hanging branch of a cottonwood tree. "We ought to cross-tie him, but poky as he is, I think this will work."

"Shall I start?" Chip hopefully asked, picking up the end of the hose.

"Hm-m-m. We need warm water, so let's get some from the house. We could use the buckets . . . and your wagon."

They soon established a system. Jenny half-filled the buckets with hot water from the kitchen and set them in the wagon, which the children pulled to the tree. After adding a little cold water from the hose, they all scrubbed the horse, using liquid soap from the sink—not Lorelei's shampoo. The routine seemed to go on forever. Dip the brush. Pour on some soap.

Scrub it round and round. Rinse it off with clean warm water. And then dip and scrub again. Before long she was nearly as wet as the horse, and Chip and Lissie left puddles wherever they stepped.

"It would be quicker just to use the hose," Lissie suggested, wiping a drip from her chin. Her tilted blue eyes were sparkling.

"Better not," Jenny decided. "That water feels like ice cubes."

They worked on. Dip—scrub—sponge.

"Why, you must have been pretty once," Jenny said. "I've never seen marks like these. Look here, kids." She pointed out narrow white streaks that ran from each front hoof up the inside of the leg. "They're unusual. And his forehead star is peculiar, too—a pair of little curving marks, one on each side."

"With a teeny stripe between," said Lissie. "And look! He likes to be scratched!" she added with a giggle.

Except for an occasional stamp, Horse was standing very still. He closed his eyes with a grunt of satisfaction when Jenny scraped at his back, blew a long noisy sigh when Lissie scrubbed his stomach, turned his head from side to side to watch the children work on his shoulders. He's actually a nice old thing, Jenny thought, as she gave the tail one last sudsing. Some day she'd pick it out hair by hair the way they did for show horses. But she couldn't manage that today.

"And now—we're through," she finally said. "Does your Mom have some beach towels? The breeze is so chilly he might take cold." She should have thought of that sooner and have had them ready.

"I'll help you look," said Lissie. "Coming, Chip?"

"Nope. I've got to let my rabbits out to play."

Jenny and the little girl rushed into the kitchen. "Just some big towels. Old ones will be all right," Jenny said in reply to Mrs. Wilson's interested question.

"Well now, of course he needs drying off," Mrs. Wilson said with a comfortable chuckle. "We can't let him catch cold."

"Mommie has lots of big towels," said Lissie, "but they aren't unpacked."

"We'll just start hunting." Mrs. Wilson puffed her way up the stairs. "Sheets—towels—all that—are packed together, and they're right here in the hall. We'll find them." Fanning her face with her handkerchief, she opened one box after another, and finally lifted out a pile of large towels.

"We'll take the worst ones," Jenny suggested. "And we've got to hurry."

"Right ho," Mrs. Wilson cheerfully agreed.

But just as they started down the stairs, they heard a scream. "Oh-h-h-h!" It rose and fell like a siren.

"Chip!" Lissie exclaimed.

"Oh-h-h!" the voice wailed again. "Jenny! Come he-e-ere!"

They pounded out the back door and raced down the path to the barn, where Chip stood with his mouth wide open, yelling at the top of his lungs. But the horse was gone. Only the frayed end of the rope was left on the tree.

"Chip. Are you all right?" Jenny demanded, putting her hands on his shoulders. "Did you get kicked?"

Still wailing, he shook his head.

"Did something frighten Horse?"

Another wail, not quite so loud.

"Chip—listen to me—what happened?"

"Well . . ." He was struggling to speak. "He still had—some soapsuds—on his stomach." The words came between loud hiccups. "And I wanted—to clean them off."

"How?" asked Jenny, although she could guess.

"With the—with the *hose*!" He broke into fresh wails. "He didn't *like* it!"

"You mean—you squirted ice-cold water—right out of the hose—on his stomach?" Jenny was aghast. "Chip! How could you?"

Tears were streaking his woebegone face. "I didn't *mean* to!" he said. "I wanted to *help*!" He flung himself face down on the ground. "I'm just du-u-umb!"

Jenny knelt beside him. She'd said too much—as usual. "Chip—stop crying! We'll get him back."

"We can't—we *can't*. We *never* will," he sobbed, clutching her with his slim little arms.

She cuddled him close. "After all," she soothed in her best baby-sitting voice, "Horse is tame. He'll probably come right to us." She tried to stand up, but he clung fast. "Let go, Chip. I have to start, before Horse gets too far away."

"That's right." Every inch the disgusted big sister, Lissie tried to pull Chip loose. "Don't forget, Chip Burnett, this is all your fault."

"I kno-o-ow!"

"So you just keep quiet and let loose of Jenny." Still he held her fast.

"I'll take him." It was the reassuring voice of Mrs. Wilson, who had followed them outside. "Here, young fellow. This is no way to behave." She laid her plump hands on Chip's shoulder, but he jerked away.

What now, thought Jenny? Pull him off by force, when he's so frightened? "Chip—you can help," she suggested. "You and Lissie and Mrs. Wilson can pin a couple of old blankets together to put over Horse when we get him back. That will keep him nice and warm."

"Is he . . . cold?" Chip asked between sobs, peeking at her from under his arm.

"He must be, wet as he is, on a morning like this." Chip's coming 'round, Jenny thought. He needs something more to do. "You can get that new rope, too. The one in the barn."

At this Chip's storm subsided as abruptly as it had begun. In a flash he was on his feet and saying well, then, he guessed he'd go after that rope right now, while Lissie put her hands on her hips and sniffed.

Free at last, Jenny considered what she should do. The escape route was obvious: down the path to the barn and through the weedy back lot, its fence in disrepair, many of its posts flat on the ground. Far beyond she could see Horse, with the rope dragging behind him—a sight that made Jenny stare in astonishment for he was actually running.

And because they lived at the edge of town, there were no houses or roads or cars or people to slow him down. Sick, coughing, soaking wet on this cold day, he was headed for the hills.

4

+++

Runaway

Some horses become quite adept at loosening knots and tripping latches. You, as handler, must look ahead, and prevent trouble.

YOU AND YOUR EQUINE FRIEND, page 139.

It couldn't be! Old Horse, of the cough and drooping head was running, actually running, not a real gallop but still so fast his tail streamed behind him. It was a nice long tail, too, dark and full.

At least the exercise will keep him warm, Jenny thought, as she pounded across the rough ground with an armful of hay. It got in her way when she let it drag and scratched her chin when she held it up, but she hung on because it was practically her only hope.

They were moving away from town toward a range of foothills, rugged and steep. If Horse ever gets into that wild country, he'll be gone for good,

Jenny thought. But look! Was he slowing down?
Yes, he'd stopped, and—oh, no! He was on the
ground and rolling in the dust, with all four legs
waving in the air.

"Horse!" Jenny wailed. "We just washed you!
What a *mess*!"

After one last wrenching wiggle, Horse rolled onto
his stomach, thrust out his front feet, and lurched to
an upright position, then raced on again. Jenny ran
too, stumbling sometimes, falling once, but quickly
up again and away, over the hard-packed earth, past
scraggly shrubs and mats of small yellow flowers. A
magpie squawked and skittered across her path, and
a brown ball of tumbleweed came rolling along.

Again Horse stopped to nibble a bunch of weeds,
and this time he let Jenny come close. She held out
the hay . . . jiggled it in the most alluring way she
could manage, while he flicked his ears and went on
eating. She crept forward, so near she could see the
smears of brown mud on his coat. But just as she was
reaching for the broken rope, which still dangled
from the halter, another huge ball of tumbleweed
whirled over the ground and bumped Horse's hind
leg. He snorted, jumped, loped away, and Jenny was
left behind.

"Horse . . . Horse . . . you crazy ninny . . . I only
want to take care of you," she gasped. Her lungs
were bursting. She couldn't run much farther. Maybe
Chip was right, and they'd never catch him, after all.

But what was that? At the sound of hoofbeats, she

turned around and saw a girl racing toward her on a shiny sorrel. Pulling up with a scuffle of dust, the girl jerked off her broad-brimmed hat and let down a mop of curly, red hair that almost matched her horse. "You've got trouble!" she exclaimed in a high, penetrating voice. "Need some help?" She was exceedingly thin, with milk-white skin and masses of freckles.

"Help! Well, I guess!" Jenny replied. "That's my horse headed for the hills."

"I know. I was over there on the road when he took off. How come he got away?"

"He broke the rope. I gave him a bath, and—" Worried as Jenny was, she didn't want to blame a little kid like Chip. "He ran off. And this wind is so cold. Is Wyoming always like this?"

"Hm-m—mornings are, this early in summer. We had frost one day last week. But afternoons warm up." The girl tapped her crop against her leather boot. "If he's had a bath, he's wet. And muddy.

"*I'll* say he's muddy."

"But we'd better get him under cover, or you'll have a sick animal on your hands." She glanced at Jenny's hay. "Goodies, I see. Is he the kind that it takes practically a posse to catch?"

"I don't know. I've never tried before."

"Well . . ." The girl plopped her hat back onto her head. "You *should* have a bucket of grain, but hay's better than nothing." Her horse pawed the ground, and she pulled him up short with a crisp, "Easy,

Rocky." When he was quiet again, she said, "Hop up behind the saddle. Let's see. . . ." She looked around. "There's a big stone. Climb on that and mount from there."

A regular Aunt Evelyn! Jenny thought with a prickle of resentment. *Bossing me around.* But she was so relieved to have help that she meekly clambered to the boulder and then to the horse's back, still clutching the hay.

"Hang on, now. When Rocky takes off, he really goes," the girl ordered. "Okay?"

"Just fine." Jenny clung tightly to her waist, the girl gave a kick and a cluck, and they bounded ahead, with Jenny's feet dangling and Rocky warm beneath her.

By now Horse had stopped to nibble a bunch of grass. "S-s-st." The girl slowed Rocky to a walk, which made him toss his head and flare his nostrils. "Easy, boy," she murmured as he minced quietly ahead.

They had drawn quite close, when he neighed, at which Horse looked up. *Oh no!* thought Jenny. *He'll start running again.* But instead he whinnied a reply and pointed his ears. "Jump off—carefully—don't step on anything that snaps," the girl whispered, coming to a halt.

Jenny slid to the ground.

"Walk toward him. Slowly. Without any noise or jerks. Runaway horses are easy to spook."

Jenny tiptoed one step at a time, pausing before

each to examine the ground for twigs. Shadows were sharp and black in the sunshine. The only sounds were the flutter of leaves in the wind and the rustle of her hay. When Horse shook his head and took a cautious step toward her, she stood as if frozen. Her heart was pounding and she hardly dared breathe.

Horse moved another step . . . another . . . stretched out his head . . . began to nibble the hay. Jenny inched it back. He took another step, and she could see the black fringe of his eyelashes.

Again he stepped forward. In slow motion, she reached her free hand under his chin. She touched the halter—curled her fingers around it—tightened her hold—and the horse was hers. But before leading him away, she dropped the hay and slid her hand along the rope, so he could devour every delicious bite. She wouldn't spoil his trust in people, not if she could help it.

"Neat!" the girl said when Jenny turned around and started to lead Horse toward her. "But . . ." She broke off, staring. "*Who*, for Pete's sake, has been taking care of that bag of bones? He looks like . . ." She stopped.

"I have!" Jenny exclaimed, lifting her chin. "But only since yesterday. I haven't had time yet to get him fattened up."

"I guess not!" The girl gathered up her reins. "Well, we'll fix that, soon enough. Can you ride him bareback?"

"I don't think so." Jenny slid her hand up the rope

until she held it just under the horse's chin. "I didn't bring a bridle. Actually, I've never been on his back, not even once."

"Sit behind me, and lead him?" The girl narrowed her eyes, which were reddish-brown, almost as bright as her hair. "No—you don't know him well enough, and your rope's rotten."

"I think—I'll just walk," Jenny suggested. As she came close, Rocky snorted, and shook his head, but Horse merely rolled his eyes and coughed again.

They moved slowly along, with Jenny holding the lead-rope and the strange girl riding beside her. "Hey! I haven't even told you my name. It's Pamela Winokur," the girl said after a few steps. She wrinkled her nose. "How's that for a mouthful?"

"It's different, all right," Jenny replied with a smile.

"It's an *awful* name. I've suffered with it all my life. Teachers can't pronounce it. People can't remember it. It's too long. And it begins with a 'w,' which puts me at the tail end of lines. But just call me Pam."

Still in her high, rapid voice, she said she lived on a ranch south of town. "Plenty of kids around here ride, but all the ranch houses except ours are way out. So . . ." She shrugged. "I generally ride alone."

"Lucky for me you came along today. And thank you, Pam. I don't know what I'd have done without you."

Pam broke into a grin. "It was neat. Catching a

runaway always is." She grinned again, and her eyes crinkled to crescent-shaped slits, fringed with thick red-brown lashes. "It stirs things up."

Grinning, with her eyes squinted almost shut and her face covered with freckles, she was so skinny and energetic that Jenny couldn't help laughing. "It does at that, but most of the fun comes after it's over. My knees are still wobbly."

"Oh, sure." Pam widened her eyes again and looked at her with frank curiosity. "But you weren't in school this year. Newcomer?"

"Yes. I'm Jenny Alexander."

"Just moved in?"

"Visiting," said Jenny. And then, because Pam seemed to be waiting, she explained who her cousins were and why she was there.

"Super! Someone nearby all summer long!" Pam drew a deep breath. "We'll take a lot of trail rides. Fatten up Old Bony." Her red-brown eyes flicked briefly toward Horse, who was shuffling along behind Jenny, head low, and coughing from time to time.

"Next," Pam continued, "we'll get in shape for the rodeo—or *maybe* we will." She glanced again at Horse. "We'll have to perk him up."

Trail rides! Rodeos! *We'll* get in shape! thought Jenny, feeling as if she were having a spin on a carnival ride and didn't know how to get off. But she liked this scrawny, blunt red-haired girl, in spite of her instant plans.

"I'm willing to try," she said. "Actually, that's why I was giving him a bath. I had to start someplace, and he was too yucky-filthy to even think of riding. And then—he rolled!"

"I saw. Horses always roll when they're wet. You should have cross-tied him." Pam grinned again. "No matter. We'll give him a good brushing when he's dry."

"Fine. But he needs more than a simple cleaning up." A lot more! Like a whole new horse! Jenny thought.

"He *looks* decrepit, all right," Pam conceded. "But when he took off—he really did run." She rode quietly for a few minutes, while the horses' hoofs plopped against the soft ground. It was almost noon, the sun was beating down, and the day, which had been so cool, was rapidly turning hot. Jenny was just wondering whether Wyoming weather always changed so much, when Pam glanced at Horse again. "Is he your cousins'? Have they had him long?"

Once more Jenny stifled a spark of resentment. Did Pam think only trash would keep an animal in such condition? "Nine days. Exactly." She briefly explained about Lorelei's move and what Mr. Brown has said.

"He left a horse! Crazy! *Nobody* dumps a horse! They're too valuable. At least . . ." Another sidewise glance. "At least *most* of them are. Why, for Pete's sake, do you think he did that?"

"I haven't a glimmer." Although Jenny tried to

sound casual, as if people misplaced their horses all the time, she felt more and more uncomfortable at the flood of questions. "Lorelei tried to find out, but the Browns weren't the least bit interested," she continued. "They said we could sell him for dog food."

"Dog food! To be *slaughtered*! Gruesome!"

For a few minutes the silence was broken only by the plop of hooves. "Jenny," Pam finally said. "There must be a reason for abandoning a horse. Even Old Bony. Did you ever think. . . ." Her voice dropped almost to a whisper. "Maybe he's stolen!"

She's taking it like a game, Jenny told herself, but it isn't a game to me. "I thought of it," she replied, staring straight ahead. "Lorelei did, too."

"Is he branded?"

"No brand. I looked when I was washing him."

"Hm-m." Pam rode silently for a few minutes. "This is really crazy. Did your cousin read the lost and found?"

"Of course!" Jenny flared. "She spent a lot of money on telephone calls and put an ad in her paper, but it didn't do one single speck of good." Questions . . . and more questions, she thought. But I can't blame her, I've been asking the same ones, myself.

Trying to sound casual, she told Pam all about Lorelei's talk with the Browns, ending, "it's weird, all right, but Lorelei decided not to fight it. She's going to let me use him this summer, and then in the fall—well—she'll figure that out when the time comes."

"Might as well. Like my dad would say, it's a cold trail."

"And this . . ." Jenny gave the lead-rope an impatient tug. "This *thing* . . . is the horse I came all the way to Wyoming to ride."

She knew she sounded bitter, but she couldn't help it. She thought about her parents' trip . . . Aunt Evelyn's house . . . the interminable year when she'd saved her money like a regular miser, so she could learn to jump with Cinnabar. No Cokes. Hardly any movies. She remembered the trip on the airplane, hoping and hoping that she'd find a good horse. And then —her first look into the stall. It had been like going over the biggest drop of the biggest roller coaster ever built. She wanted to run away, or curl up by herself in a little dark hole.

"I tried not to expect too much, but . . ." She glanced again at Horse, who was shuffling along with his eyes almost closed. "Still, I can't help liking him, in a way. He's such a patient old fellow, and when we curried him, he acted as if he thought it was heaven. If—if only he weren't quite so *crummy*."

She blinked back tears. She supposed Pam would ask still more questions, as if it were an exciting book, and she couldn't wait to read it all.

Instead Pam seemed to understand, for her voice softened. "What a jolt! But maybe I can help. I'd like to—honest. I've raised orphan calves on bottles, but I've never tackled a *really* neglected horse. That will be absolutely the greatest." Squinting her eyes again, sizing up Horse like something on a bargain rack, she began to rush ahead as eagerly as before. "First, we'll fatten him up. That should make him more lively. And then—oh—lots of things. Trim his forelock. Comb his mane. Ditto his tail."

"I really do need some help," Jenny replied, with a surge of relief. It was wonderful to have a friend, even an Aunt Evelyn type.

For a few minutes they walked quietly along. "What's his name?" Pam then asked. "Or didn't that guy tell you?"

"He didn't say. And so far I can't think of anything that isn't positively stupid. His only marks are the streaks on his legs and the star. Only of course it isn't a star—just those two little curves, like a pair of crescent moons, back to back. But you wouldn't name a horse Cresent or Moon."

"Hardly," Pam agreed. She said hers was Sky Rocket, Rocky for short, because of his bright color and quick starts. "Even as a foal he'd take off in a flash."

As they walked on, Jenny drew deep breaths of the crisp air, scented with something fresh and sharp. She learned that Pam was nearly a year older and a year ahead of her in high school, that for both of them the favorite sport—next to riding—was swimming. But Jenny loved art, while Pam went in for carpentry.

"I took woodworking last term" she said. "Only girl in the class, and I made a tack box."

Just as they started comparing favorite tapes and pop groups, they heard a shrill voice. "Jenny!"

"Hi! We're over here!"

Chip and Lissie were sitting on a large gray stone, and in a moment Lissie began to sing,

> "Where it's smooth and where it's sto-ny,
> Run along, my lit-tle po-ny."

The song rang on and on until Jenny and Pam were close, when Lissie broke it off and said, "Horse came right to you. He isn't wild at all."

"Well, not very. At least when he sees some hay," Jenny replied.

Chip solemnly handed her the length of new rope. "Here," he chirped, then added, with an admiring glance at Rocky, "That's really a cool one. Is it a stallion?"

"Well—no—not exactly," Pam replied. "He's— well—"

"Ours isn't either," Chip said. "He *was* a gentleman horse, but he isn't any more. Anyway, that's what my mommie said."

"Rocky too. And now—want a ride? Hop on then. Both of you."

"Neat-oh!"

Jenny gave them each a boost, Lissie in back of Pam, Chip in front, beaming and waving an imaginary whip. They moved slowly on, with Jenny still leading Horse.

When they reached the barn, the girls tied their mounts to the rings in the wall. "Almost dry," Jenny said, laying her hand on Horse's side. "I ought to wash him again, but I can't face it. I'll just rub him down." She ran inside and came back with a couple of gunny sacks. "These ought to do."

"Sure. Once he's dry, most of the mud will brush off. Have you got a blanket?" Pam gave one of the sacks a vigorous shake.

" 'Course we have," Chip shrilled. "Me and Lissie and Mrs. Wilson pinned some camping ones together because she thought he'd be cold. I'll get them." He was off in a flash.

Jenny and Pam began to rub the muddy horse. "Is his stall ready?" Pam asked in a moment. "Big enough so he can move around? Lots of straw?"

"We've some. But . . . well . . . I'll have to get more." Jenny was thinking hard. Lorelei had bought only a little hay. Ordered small-size hamburgers last night. Had oatmeal for breakfast. And what had she said about the house? That it needed a roof and plumbing and paint job, as fast as she could get the cash? Something about a five-year plan or "more likely ten?"

So she couldn't ask Lorelei to buy a thing, especially after the way she, Jenny, had stormed at her mother and made a million promises not to be any trouble. Instead she'd use her summer's spending money—one hundred dollars—which was plenty, Mom had said, for a simple family vacation. There go my cokes and movies, she thought. And even if she spent every penny, how long would it support a horse?

She looked longingly at the bunches of coarse grass that were battling weeds in the yard beside the barn. Food! Not very much—but it was free! "I wonder, Pam . . . do you think we could mend this fence?"

Pam wiggled one of the few standing posts. "Too rickety, even if we propped it up. Takes a strong fence to hold a horse."

"Do you know anything about tying them?"

"My Dad doesn't approve." She scuffed at one of the clumps. "Still . . . that's grass, all right. Not much, but it'd be good for him, if you're careful not to let him get tangled up. Shall we give it a try?"

Fastening the longer, newer rope to Horse's halter, they led him to the grassiest spot and tied him to a reasonably solid post. "He acts as if his life depends on it," Jenny said, for Horse was eating even before they had finished the knot.

"He likes it, that's sure. But don't forget to keep watch." Pam swung into the saddle. "And now I've got to go—my mom will be wondering. Shall we ride tomorrow?"

"I'd love it. That is, if Horse is feeling okay."

"Oh he'll be better then. We'll get some grain, too. There's a feed store not far away."

Plans again, thought Jenny, but it didn't bother her now. "See you then," she replied. "And Pam—thanks again—for everything. You just about saved my life."

"Well . . . not exactly, and besides, I was having a great time. I'll think tonight about what else we can do for Horse, and I'll check the rodeo dates, too."

With a wave of her hand, Pam trotted off, while Jenny hurried into the barn. She would put on the pinned-together blanket and clean up that filthy box stall this very minute, and bed Horse down in the small one. While she was doing it, she'd figure out how to get the grain, and there must be some way to find out where he came from. Should she write to the Browns? Put an ad in the Salt Lake City paper? Put some pictures in store windows?

She giggled. Why was she worrying? She only had to wait for tomorrow, and Pam would tell her exactly what to do.

5

++

Nothing
Comes Cheap

*You are responsible not only for the shine of
your horse's coat, but also for its energy and
spirit, its very life. Obviously, you must pro-
vide a good diet.*

YOU AND YOUR EQUINE FRIEND, page 57.

"I-I-I've a little kitty at home and she
    kno-o-o-ows me.
When I come . . ."
The song broke off just as Jenny bounded out
of bed, her mind made up. She was going to spend
her money, the entire hundred dollars, if necessary,
for Horse. Throwing on her clothes, she dashed
downstairs, where she found the children at breakfast and Lorelei scribbling frantically on an oversized
note pad. Piles of paper littered the table.

"Jenny! Hail—and all that!" she said, writing as
she spoke. "There's cereal on the shelf"—scribble—

"got to get this done—deadline today." She riffled through the papers. "Worked on it last night—didn't get through—you'll have to shift for yourself."

"That's okay," Jenny assured her as she poured a bowl of cornflakes. "I think . . ." she began, but Lissie interrupted, blue eyes wide.

"S-s-sh! We've got to keep quiet. Mommie's *busy*!"

Jenny put her finger to her lips and nodded, while Lorelei flipped to another page.

The silence was abruptly broken by Honey, who scrambled up the side of his cage and squawked, "Ah-oh!" At once Lissie whirled around. "Chip! Cover him *up*! He's *bothering*!"

"Okay. Okay!" Chip crossed his eyes at Lissie, then stomped indignantly across the floor and flung a shawl over Honey's cage. "All he did was tell Jenny hello. Can't he even . . ."

"Mommie! Chip did that thing with his eyes again!"

"Hey there!" Lorelei spoke without looking up. "That's enough, Mr. Chip. And you too, Lissie." With a final sip from a brown mug, she swept her papers together, kissed the children, and dashed out the door. "Mrs. Wilson's coming," she called above the chorus of goodbyes. "I see her now."

Before her car was out of the driveway, the front door squeaked and the baby-sitter waddled into the kitchen, bringing an aroma of peppermint. "Sorry I'm so late," she said. "It was Bert—my oldest kid.

He's going out with a pack string today, and I had to take him to his base camp." She launched into a jolly account of the problems of tourists' guides.

Jenny waited as patiently as she could. "Mrs. Wilson," she said at the first lull. "Can you tell me where the nearest feed store is? And how soon it will be open?"

"Straight to Main Street—that's six blocks, maybe seven—and then left. Three . . . four blocks along. Atwater's. They open early, on account of the ranchers. Packers too." Pouring a cup of coffee, Mrs. Wilson settled down for a cozy chat. "Hard life, ranching is, even when the sun cooperates. The ranchers hate daylight savings, all of them do."

"I'm sure of that," Jenny agreed. "And now—"

Mrs. Wilson paid no attention. "Horses and cows wake up with the sun and go to bed when it's dark."

"Mrs. Wilson! Hey, Mrs. Wilson!" Chip, who had just pulled the shawl off Honey's cage, was dancing with impatience.

"Yes, Chip. Trouble?"

"I need some lettuce for my rabbits."

"Sure. Right there in the fridge. You know, well as I do." She buttered a piece of toast. "So daylight savings is all out of step with the ranches."

"Yes, I know," said Jenny. "And now . . ."

"Can't blame them. It throws everything out of kilter on a ranch, this summer time does." Mrs. Wilson drained her cup and lumbered across the floor for the coffeepot.

Jenny spoke out quickly. "Mrs. Wilson, I have to feed my horse now. I'm trying to fatten him up."

"We'll help," offered Chip, turning away from the refrigerator with a handful of lettuce. "Beat you there, Lissie!" The door banged, and the children were gone.

Jenny eagerly followed. Horse had grazed for an hour the afternoon before, had eaten a lot of hay, and had spent the night in a clean stall. Maybe, just maybe, he would be better now.

As she swung open the barn door, she listened but heard only the rustle of straw. No cough. No labored breathing. "Feeling better, old fellow?" she asked, slipping in beside him and holding out her hand. He snorted softly and nuzzled into it, then rubbed his head against her arm with a contented sigh.

"He *likes* you, Jenny," exclaimed Lissie, standing on the box.

"I want to feel his nose too!" Chip demanded. "Let's saddle him up and take a ride."

"We have to take care of him first," Jenny reminded them. "See—his hay's all gone, and his water, too. And then I'm going to the store to buy some supplies."

"We'll go with you." Chip clambered down from the box.

"Not this time. It's too far." Seeing the set of his jaw, Jenny hastily added, "But soon as we're sure Horse is well, I'll give you a ride every day."

"Honest?" Chip's scowl vanished.

"Cross my heart."

"Okay. We're going to Tim and Terry's house anyway." These were new friends who lived across the street. "They've got a whole set of swings and stuff." Both children were away in a flash.

Twenty minutes later Jenny was ready to leave. It was a bright morning but cool under the fir trees that lined the sidewalk. She stared at the houses, painted white, with boxy front porches and spacious lawns. Sprinklers were whirling; some little girls were playing hopscotch; a small boy was pulling a red wagon full of rocks.

Half a mile along she came to Main Street, which was very broad, with brown buildings along both sides, shaded by wide wooden awnings. "Cowboy Cafe" said the sign on one, and "The Tack Man" on another.

Turning right, she soon found the feed store, big and dusty, with shelves of vitamins and supplies, and feed in an adjoining shed. "I need some wood shavings," she told the clerk. "For one horse, but I'm not sure how much."

"Shavings? Oh—you mean for the stall. We use straw here." He was a wiry young man, not very tall, with a big hat pushed far back on his head.

"All right, straw then. Is is very expensive?"

"Not expensive at all. To last how long?"

"Well . . . about a month." Better be conservative, she thought.

"A month. Say about three bales?"

"Yes—that will be fine."

The man suggested something of good quality, without any oat-straw in it. "So he won't eat his bedding. Some horses do that, you know."

"Of course." Jenny tried to look as if she knew all about the eating habits of Horse. "I need some hay, too."

"Now? In the summer?"

"I'm afraid so," Jenny sadly told him. "We have just a little bit of grass, sort of a back lot that's mostly weeds."

"Okay. Alfalfa hay, I suppose. Two bales?" The young man was writing it down.

"And grain. My horse really needs pepping up."

"M-m-m. How about feeding him a good grain mix for half, and a high-protein mix for the other half? It has extra vitamins, too. Say about fifty pounds of each, and see how he does."

"Well—yes. That sounds right." It sounds a lot, Jenny thought.

"Fifty pounds grain, fifty pounds hi-pro mix," the young man murmured, writing again. "That'll do you a little more than a month. Now—a salt block? Got to give your horse salt if you want to keep him healthy. And it won't set you back a bundle, either."

"Yes, of course. A salt block."

"White or red?" Tucking his pencil behind his ear, he led her to a shelf where salt blocks were sitting in a precise row. "Red's better. Has more minerals."

"Red then." Jenny felt as if she were dreaming

about a fall into a bottomless pit, down and down and down, and no matter how far she went, there was always farther still to go.

"One manger block red salt." The salesman had his pencil poised again. "Some soybean oil meal? It helps shed out the winter coat. Keeps a horse glossy."

"Well . . . let's see how much . . ."

"Sure thing." He added his figures and Jenny gasped. It couldn't be! It was way over half of her money, and it would last only a month! She'd have to get some baby-sitting jobs, or *something*.

"That's . . . quite a lot more than I expected," she stammered. "Can I cut it down?"

"Sure," he cheerfully said. "Best place to cut is the high-pro mix. Make it one part in four instead of half and half. Your animal will still do all right, even though he won't pick up quite so fast."

"Okay. How much will it be?"

This time the sum was more reasonable, so she pulled her wallet out of her jeans pocket. "No—nothing more," she said, keeping her voice resolutely firm, although it wanted to wobble. "This will be all for a start. How will I get them home?"

"We'll deliver, but we're snowed right now. Thursday be okay?" the salesman asked.

"Thursday? That's fine," Jenny replied as she stuffed the change into her wallet. At this rate, she'd need a fortune.

Mrs. Wilson had made broccoli soup for lunch, which Jenny generally loved, but today it tasted like paste. When everything cost so much, how was she going to feed Horse for the whole summer? Leaving half of her soup, she wandered disconsolately to the barn, picked up the saddle and one of the blankets, and pulled the bridle off its hook. She'd tack him up and have a short ride, at least. But these contraptions had so many buckles! And a great big bit with a crook in it!

While she was trying to figure it out, she heard her name and rushed outside to find that Pam had just come down the lane. "Ready for a ride?" she called as she slid off Rocky's back, and unstrapped the blanket.

"Well . . . just about."

"I told my dad all about your horse. He said we ought to advertise—*if* the animal is any good. But when I told him how he looks . . ." She glanced at Horse and rolled her eyes.

We ought to advertise, thought Jenny, half irritated, half amused. Just as if she owned him.

"Now—first thing we'll go to the feed store," Pam continued, handing over the blanket.

"I've already been," Jenny replied and grinned at Pam's blink of surprise. She listed the things she had bought, then said, "And Pam, I'm really glad you've come, because I'm perishing for a ride, and I'm not sure which way this silly bit goes."

Pam looked surprised. "Didn't they teach you to saddle up at your riding academy?"

"I learned it—sure—for the kind of tack I'm used to." Did Pam think she was a complete dummy!

"Oh—of course—you ride English. One of those teeny saddles with short stirrups and no horn."

"Naturally. Everybody does, where I live."

Pam shrugged. "Well . . . they ride English in shows at Salt Lake and the state fair and a few other places, but it wouldn't be much good on a ranch. So —let's see if this is all here."

Gingerly taking the bridle, she held it at arm's length and wrinkled her nose. "Ugh! Has it *ever* been cleaned? The leather's stiff as a board. And *what's* on the bit?" It was caked with something Jenny didn't even like to think about. "Well . . . where's the nearest water? And a brush?"

"Water? At the house. I'll get some." She raced away and returned with a bucketful.

"It's a curb bit," Pam explained as they began to scrub. "The only kind for a rodeo. I expect you'll catch on."

"I expect I will," Jenny replied, gritting her teeth. If riding here meant using this stuff—then she'd use it. She hadn't come all the way to Wyoming for nothing.

As soon as the bridle was clean, they brought Horse outside, along with the rest of his gear. Privately Jenny thought the bit looked cruel, and the saddle enormously large and heavy. But I won't say a word, she told herself. Grumbling won't help.

Working together, they soon had Horse ready, and Jenny eagerly mounted. "It's so stiff! I can hardly feel the horse!" she said, sliding back and forth in the saddle. "And these stirrups are practically buckets!" She bent sidewise to shorten a leather.

"Jenny!" Pam was scandalized. "That's a mile and a half too *short*! Is *that* the way you ride?"

"Of course. So I can bend my knees."

"Well, we don't *crouch!*" Pam was busily letting the stirrup down again. "There. That's better."

Jenny put in her feet and tried to assume the relaxed position she had seen in pictures. But Pam began to laugh.

"For Pete's sake! You're leaning way back. Like a souped-up motorcycle."

"I'm *trying* to do it your way," Jenny replied, rather curtly. "So I look ridiculous." Know-it-all Pam, she thought, and immediately reminded herself, That's not fair. She's trying to help.

But when she looked at her own feet, thrust forward with the toes turned up, she laughed, too. "I must be a sight," she agreed. "But I've always had to sit straight and keep my heels down and my elbows in and hold my hands low and all that. So now . . ."

"So now you've stuck your feet out halfway to Horse's chin!" Pam was still giggling. "Try pulling them back, and rest against your cantle—the lower part of your back. Let yourself sort of rock back and forth as the horse goes. Relaxed." She watched as Jenny tried again. "That's pretty good now."

"I'll never get used to it. Never," Jenny said. "And Horse acts as if he doesn't like it either. Look at him!" He was tugging at the reins and twisting his head.

"No wonder, the way you're sawing at his mouth," Pam told her. "Put both reins in one hand—looser. Don't *pull*. Just lay them sidewise across his neck. He'll turn all right."

Jenny tried again, and after a few rounds of the weedy lot felt she was catching on. And now she was ready to ride at last.

However, instead of mounting Rocky, Pam stood motionless, arms akimbo. "Jenny, you forgot something."

Jenny looked at her reins—her heels—her knees. "I . . . I don't . . ."

"Check his feet! You ought to hear my dad on the subject of horses' feet." She had squatted down and was squinting one eye at Horse. "Walk him a little."

Jenny anxiously did as she was told.

"I thought so." Pam stood up. "He's favoring his left front foot. Let's have a look." Lifting it, she eyed it closely, then bent her head and sniffed. "See—it's red. Smells bad, too. If he has thrush, that's serious."

Jenny shuddered. "It looks perfectly awful! I'll get it taken care of, soon as I can."

"Soon as you *can*? You'd better do it *right away*! We'll call my dad's vet—Dr. Mike Santoro. He's *neat*. Shall we telephone now?"

"Well—later."

"Why not now, for Pete's sake? He's coughing

again, too. We had a horse once with a cough like that, and my dad had the vet come every day. But he still kept getting worse and worse . . . until he died."

"*Pam! Not really!*" Jenny gasped. But what could she do when she didn't even have enough money for the summer's food? "Maybe he'll get better, now that I'm feeding him more," she hopefully suggested. "Anyway, I'm going to wait, at least a day or so."

"And besides that, he ought to be shod. Look how long his hoofs are. No wonder he's going lame."

"I can see. I'm not *entirely* dense," Jenny flared. "But just the same, I'll have to wait until—until I've figured things out."

Pam shrugged. "Well . . . okay. I suppose you have to check with your cousin. Just don't forget—Dr. Mike Santoro. He's a good one."

"I won't forget. But I don't think I'll ride after all, until Horse is better. I don't want to make him worse."

"I agree. I ought to be getting home anyway. We spent an awful lot of time cleaning the tack." After giving Jenny an additional flood of advice, Pam rode away.

The rest of the day dragged. Jenny watched Horse graze and studied the chapter on diseases in *You and Your Equine Friend*, which only frightened her more. Wrote a letter to her parents. Made a dozen trips to the barn to look at the sore foot, but found it no better.

It must really hurt, and he's coughing more all the time, she told herself. *I shouldn't have ridden him, even in the yard. Pam's right—he needs a doctor. But I can't ask Lorelei to pay for it, after all my promises to Mom.*

Then a terrible thought came to her. She tried to banish it, tried to call it impossible and grandiose and out of the question and altogether-to-much-to-expect. But no matter how many times she pushed it away, it cropped up again.

You've a lot of money in the bank at home. You could get it, the same as your dad gets money when he's on his trips. Then you could pay the vet.

No! She almost said it aloud. It's for lessons on Cinnabar.

Suppose you spend it. Maybe your parents will let you take the lessons anyway.

Fat chance! Mom believes in teaching me Responsibility and Thrift. If I use that money, it'll be no Cinnabar in the fall. So I'll keep it.

No matter how sick Horse is? Maybe he'll die.

I know! I know!

She wandered around the house, straightening a picture, stacking the magazines. She tried to draw a sketch of the hills, but tore it up. She wished Lissie and Chip were there. They'd had a game of Animal Lotto last evening, which had dragged on absolutely forever, but now she'd be glad to play even that.

"Goodness, Jenny," Mrs. Wilson said, looking up

from the table she was polishing with something that smelled like pine. "You're nervous as a cat. Is something wrong, honey?"

"Not really."

"I made peanut butter cookies—you might sample them. There's nothing like food, I always say, to settle the nerves. It works for me, every time."

"No thank you. I'm not a bit hungry."

"They'd be a nice little snack with milk." Mrs. Wilson put the cap back on the polish can. "Actually, I'd like some myself. We might just have us a little tea party. I'll put the kettle on." She waddled into the kitchen, with Jenny at her heels.

"Mrs. Wilson, I know the cookies are really good and I'm really sorry not to have them but I'm going out for a while," she said all in one breath. "I'll be back before long." Before the baby-sitter could answer, she bolted out the front door.

That morning, on her way to the feed store, she had passed a branch of her own home bank, and all day the memory had followed her around like a troublesome little dog. It was only four o'clock . . . plenty of time to get there before it closed. Half against her will, she started down the now-familiar street and in ten minutes slipped through the swinging glass door.

Once inside the dim, quiet room, she hesitated feeling as if she had suddenly shrunk to the size of Chip. Always before, when she'd gone to a bank, she'd been with her mother and simply tagged along.

But now—should she stand in that line? Go to those high counters? She decided on the line and soon was facing a smiling girl behind the grill of a teller's window.

"I have some money in another branch of this bank, and I want to send for it," she said, trying to sound as if she had financial transactions all the time.

"To withdraw funds from a member bank?" the girl replied. "You should see one of our officers for that. Right over there." She pointed to an open space behind a railing, where several people were working at flat-topped desks.

"Oh—thank you. Thank you very much." Keeping her back stiff, Jenny walked to the railing and waited until a woman beckoned. Maybe it would be easier to say it now.

The sign on the woman's desk said Lois Andrews, and she didn't look at all like Jenny's idea of a bank officer, being middle-aged and thin, with dangling earrings and a huge purple ring.

"Is it in your name only?" she asked when Jenny explained her errand. "Or do your parents have to sign with you when you withdraw it?" She examined a chipped place in her nail polish.

"I—don't know. I've never taken any out. Just put it in." *And in. And in, All year long.* Jenny felt hollow clear to her toes.

"You have identification? From your branch, I mean."

"A bank card. It's in my wallet," said Jenny, handing it over. She stood first on one foot and then the other while Mrs. Andrews read it slowly, pursing her lips. Typewriters were clicking and people were talking in low voices.

"I see. With your account number. All in order." The woman copied the information. "How much do you have?" she asked.

"Nearly three hundred dollars."

"So much?" Mrs. Andrews opened a drawer and took out a printed form, then waited quietly, apparently for an explanation, so Jenny hastily added, "I earned some of it baby-sitting and got some for my birthday and some for Christmas."

After a piercing gaze through her shiny glasses, Mrs. Andrews inserted the form into her typewriter. "Your name? Address? Age?" The keys clicked as she also recorded Lorelei's name and address, and how they were related.

When Jenny had answered the questions, the woman hesitated. "Jenny—why do you want your money?" she suddenly asked.

"I—need it," Jenny replied. Hadn't she explained enough?

"I really ought to have a reason."

"Just to get my own money?" Jenny was sure her dad drew funds when he was on trips, without all this trouble.

"Well . . ." Mrs. Andrews began to tap her desk with the finger that wore the purple ring. "I would much prefer that you had someone to sign with you. Your cousin?"

"Oh, no! I don't want to bother her!" Jenny exclaimed. "Why do I have to have somebody sign, when it belongs to me?"

There was a long pause while the woman's bright brown eyes seemed to look straight into Jenny's brain. *What's she thinking?* Jenny wondered. *Doesn't she want to give me my own money?* "I'll see what I can do," Mrs. Andrews said then, pulling the form out of the typewriter. "As soon as I have a reply, I'll let you know. Probably tomorrow."

"I thought I'd get it today. My dad—"

"No. Tomorrow. We'll telephone."

A few minutes later Jenny was outside the door.

When she returned home, Chip and Lissie were waiting for her. "Shall we play Animal Lotto again?" Chip asked. "I've figured out some neat prizes."

"Not now," Jenny replied. "I'm going upstairs and read for a while." Seeing how disappointed they looked, she added more gently, "We'll play later on." She needn't be mean to a couple of little kids just because her own life was crosswise.

Upstairs, she pulled out her sketch pad from the drawer and slowly leafed through it. There was Cinnabar jumping—Cinnabar in his stall—herself on his back. Her pictures. Her dreams.

The sketch pad slipped from her fingers as she flung herself onto the bed. How could things be so wrong! She had only Chip and Lissie for company, and sometimes Pam—but Pam was a stranger, and bossy besides. And Lorelei was so busy—and the horse so sick and old. She'd been here only three days, but she was already tired of jagged hills and sagebrush and crummy old houses that needed repairs. Tired of worrying about hay and grain and vets and horse-shoes. She wanted to see palm trees and bougainvillea and red tile roofs. To walk on the beach. Go to the movies with her friends. Have a swim in their pool, and—yes—take a ride on Melody.

She picked up the picture of Cinnabar. "Horse is sick," she told him, half aloud. "He may die, and there's only me to help him. It will take all my money, I think. Everything I've been saving for practically forever. So . . . when fall comes . . . and I get back home . . . I won't have any left. I won't be able to take jumping lessons on you after all."

Farfalla

Horses are subject to many kinds of illness, some of which are serious. As owner and/or trainer, you must be alert for the danger symptoms.

YOU AND YOUR EQUINE FRIEND, page 78.

Promptly at ten o'clock the next morning, the time the bank opened, Jenny curled up with her book on the living room floor, close to the hall telephone. Horse was worse today, so she had decided to call Pam's veterinarian the very minute the money came. She had his number now, on a slip of paper. *Why didn't it ring?*

From where she sat Jenny could see the tall clock, with its relentlessly swinging pendulum and hands that seemed to scarcely move at all. "Shall we play a game?" she asked when Lissie came skipping past with the Lotto box in her arms.

The little girl shook her head. "We're going to Tim and Terry's house and stay for lunch. Their mommie invited us yesterday. But we'll play with you this afternoon." She trotted away.

Serves me right, thought Jenny. I've wished so often that they'd leave me alone—and now they're doing it. But today their chatter and squabbles, even their dumbest games, would be better than waiting around all by herself. Everything was still except the ticking of the clock and assorted bumps from above as Mrs. Wilson moved packing boxes around upstairs.

Suddenly the telephone jangled, and Jenny snatched it up, but it was only Pam. "Strawberries are ready sooner than we expected," she explained. "So I've got to pitch in. My Mom and I run a regular jam factory. I can't come until tomorrow."

"Oh—well—okay," Jenny replied. She kept the conversation short, so as not to tie up the line.

Eleven o'clock came, and Jenny darted down the path to the barn, running both ways so she wouldn't miss the call. Eleven-thirty, and she visited Horse again, finding him no better. Twelve, and she dragged through lunch, with Mrs. Wilson amiably explaining the virtues of vitamins.

By two o'clock she was wandering restlessly around the house, feeling sure her money must be there by now and Mrs. Andrews had forgotten to let her know. She wouldn't wait another minute, but would get it in person.

"I'm going down town for a while," she told Mrs. Wilson. "I'll be back before dinner."

"Problems?" Mrs. Wilson eagerly asked. "You know, I'm supposed to take care of whatever you kiddies need, and I'm ready and willing. Lorelei said—"

Rude as she knew it was, Jenny interrupted. "Thank you, Mrs. Wilson. You've already helped me a lot with Horse's blanket. But I can handle this all right."

Nobody else, nobody but me, can take care of it, she told herself as she plunged out the door.

This time the bank didn't look so strange, and she went directly to the desk of Mrs. Andrews, who was wearing the purple ring again. Jenny stood quietly until she looked up.

"I've come for my money," Jenny began. "It must be here by now."

Mrs. Andrews stopped typing. "So soon? Jenny, these things take time. We've had a little delay, but we expect to hear from your home branch tomorrow." Her forehead puckered in the faintest hint of a frown. "Is your problem urgent? Perhaps I can help you more, if you'll explain."

"Oh, no. It isn't urgent. Not at all," Jenny hastily said. She'd have to escape quickly because Mrs. Andrews was eying her again with that gimlet look. "It's no big deal . . . I just—I was wondering . . . And thank you . . . thank you very much . . ." Still murmuring thanks, she fled.

So much for that! she thought, as she walked swiftly toward home. Horse could die without any medicine, for all any of them cared. And then she realized that she couldn't expect people to help her when she hadn't told them what was wrong.

But I can't explain. If I do, they'll tell Lorelei, she reminded herself. *And I promised and promised not to bother her. I've got to figure it out on my own.*

At home she visited the stable again and found that Horse's cough was deeper and that he was limping more. She led him slowly outside and tied him up, hoping the grass would have lots of vitamins and do him more good than hay. Maybe tomorrow, when his supplies were delivered, the Hi-Pro mix would help.

On her way back to the house she met Lissie and Chip, who had just come home and were crawling on the ground, each with a glass jar. "We're hunting insects," Lissie explained.

"For my tadpoles," Chip proudly added. "See. I've caught two flies already. Want to help us?"

"Well, not right now. I've tied Horse up, so he can have some grass," Jenny replied, "and I have to get him some water."

"I'll get it. We can hardly find any bugs anyway," Lissie exclaimed, springing to her feet.

"But we *have* to! Or my tadpoles will *starve*! You don't want them to be *hungry*, do you?"

"I'll help you, just as soon as I get the water,"

Jenny offered. "I have to stay close by, anyway, and watch Horse."

"Neat-oh!" Chip replied. "Now we'll catch a lot."

An hour later, with four lady bugs, two flies, and a grasshopper safely in the jars, Jenny untied Horse and led him slowly back to his stall. He stumbled once, and he was coughing again.

"I wish we had a name for him," Lissie said as she walked beside Jenny. "He's so pretty. Can you think of a good one?"

"I've thought and thought," Jenny replied, shaking her head. "And nothing is just right. He hasn't any marks that mean anything, and he's too sick and poky to do funny little tricks. Nothing to give me a single idea."

"Just those two little curves on his forehead," Lissie agreed.

"Curvey?" suggested Chip. "Clam shell?"

"Chip! That's *dumb*!" Lissie was properly disgusted.

"It looks a little bit like a butterfly," Jenny reflected.

"Oh—Butterfly!" Lissie clapped her hands together. "Can we name him that?"

"Do you think it sounds—well—solid enough for a horse?" Jenny asked as she put him into his stall.

"M-m-m, I guess not. But it's pretty. And it's all the mark he has."

"Except those stripes on his legs, and they hardly show," added Chip. "We could call him Stripie."

"Stripie!" Lissie pursed her lips.

But her earlier comment had started Jenny thinking. "Butterfly—I wonder what that is in Spanish. Cinnabar has sort of a Spanish sound. Does your mother have any foreign language dictionaries?" At Lissie's puzzled expression, Jenny started to explain what they were, then said, "Let's see what we can find in her books. Will it be all right to borrow them?"

"She won't care. She says books are to use."

"Beat you!" Chip shouted and led the way to the house.

Although a double row of packing boxes still cluttered Lorelei's bedroom, her electric typewriter was in place on an oversized desk, beside a rumpled stack of paper. "Mommie's book," Lissie proudly explained. "She let me read some of it once. It has real big words."

Many of the boxes held books, and Jenny soon found an unabridged dictionary with foreign language supplements at the back.

"Perfect!" she said, sitting on the edge of the bed and balancing the bulky volume on her lap, while the children leaned on her from both sides. "Buttercup . . . butterfat . . . Here it is in Spanish. Butterfly. *Mariposa*."

"That's pretty, like a song," said Lissie. "He could be Merry for short. Or Posy."

Chip's voice dripped scorn. "Posy! For a *man horse*?"

"I think you're right, Chip," Jenny agreed. "Let's see what else we can find." She turned to the French section. "Here—Butterfly: *Papillon*. How do you like that?" She hoped her pronunciation was somewhere near correct.

"*Papillon*. That's pretty, too," Lissie declared.

"We could call him Pappy," Chip added.

"Well . . ." Jenny tried not to laugh, but Lissie interrupted.

"Not *Pappy!* He's a *boy horse* all right. But he isn't anybody's *daddy*."

"That's so. We'll look again."

The next, German, was *Schmetterling*. "Smetter—shmetter—," the children tried, and Jenny's attempt was almost as awkward. "We'll never get our tongues around that," she said with a giggle. "And what would we use for a nickname?"

"Schmetty? Schmelly?" shrieked Chip, shaking with laughter.

"Lingy?" asked Lissie. "No, Jenny. That word—that smetter—well, I don't like that at *all*."

"There's only one left," Jenny said. "Italian." She flipped through the pages. "Hey—how about this? *Farfalla*."

"Falla sounds like a man. Almost like *fellow*," suggested Chip.

"And *far*," Lissie said. "He can run far. At least, I *think* he can. When he gets well."

"*Farfalla*. I really do like it," Jenny said, trying the name again. "We'll see what your mother says, but

I'm almost sure that will be it. *Farfalla*—Butterfly—for his star." It was a perfect name—romantic like Cinnabar.

"Can we ride him?" asked Lissie. "I didn't have a ride on—on—Farfalla—yet."

"Not today," Jenny firmly said. "I'm going to let him rest and get over that cough. His foot's sore, too. Besides, it's almost time for your mother to come home, and we'll want to see how she likes the new name."

They wandered into the kitchen and settled at the round table for a game, while Mrs. Wilson grated cabbage for cole slaw. "Mind you watch him," she cautioned Chip, when he opened the cage and set Honey on his shoulder. "I found him loose this morning, and he'd torn open the bread wrapper."

"He likes to be out," Chip replied. "He won't do anything bad. Can I feed him?"

"Sure. Want some meat?" A large kettle was simmering on the stove, and Mrs. Wilson forked a few morsels from it onto a saucer.

Grinning, Chip held up a piece for the bird to take from his fingers. "Honey likes meat," he said. "Hey! Ouch!"

"Bite you?"

"It hardly hurt at all," Chip stoutly replied. Sucking his finger, he set the saucer on the floor, with Honey beside it.

But as time passed, and Lorelei hadn't appeared,

the children grew restless. "Where's Mommie?" Chip asked.

She's *never* this late," Lissie agreed.

"Now don't you fret," Mrs. Wilson reassured them. "Remember what a hurry she was in this morning. She's just had an extra lot of work to do today. She'd have called us, don't worry, if anything went wrong." She began to sing *My Darling Clementine* in a loud voice, urging the children to join in.

However, by the time the clock struck six, Mrs. Wilson was uneasy too, standing beside the window with the curtain drawn back.

"I want Mommie to come. She's *awful* late!" whimpered Chip.

"And she didn't even telephone," Lissie added. "She always telephones."

"Now never you mind. I won't go off and leave you kiddies alone. Your mother knows that, and she knows you're all right." Waddling to the stove, Mrs. Wilson noisily tasted the contents of the kettle. "And I've cooked you up a good stew, so your dinner will be ready whenever she comes."

"I'll read you a story. Would you like some *Winnie the Pooh*?" suggested Jenny.

"All right," Chip agreed, but just then Lorelei appeared.

"No. No problems," she said, as she wrapped them in a hug, then shooed them to the bathroom to wash their hands. But all during the meal she kept looking at Jenny with troubled eyes.

Later on, when Chip and Lissie were tucked into bed and Jenny was reading in her own room, Lorelei came to the door, and as before, asked to come in.

"Okay," said Jenny, laying down the book and moving over so her cousin could sit beside her on the bed. Lorelei clearly had something to say. Probably, thought Jenny, something she wouldn't like.

For a minute Lorelei sat quietly with her hands clasped, then drew a deep breath. "Jenny, I have to talk with you," she said.

Jenny stared at her book.

"It's about—you see, Jenny, in a place like Pine Valley, everybody knows everybody, and . . ."

"So—?" Jenny was puzzled. Had she broken some silly small-town rule?

"Mrs. Andrews, from the bank, telephoned me today," Lorelei continued. "She asked me to drop in there this afternoon. That's why I was so late."

Suddenly Jenny realized what it was. "Has the crummy old bank been telling tales?" she demanded, sitting up very straight. "I thought what you told a bank was *confidential*." Had they figured out what she wanted? If they had, would Lorelei think she had to pay all those costs?

"There's nothing to worry about," Lorelei hastily assured her. "Mrs. Andrews was just concerned because you're a minor and wanted all that money and wouldn't tell her what for."

"That doesn't give her the right to repeat—"

"Jenny—she knew you were visiting me—you told her that. So she thought I ought to know, and contacted me, not so much as a bank officer as a neighbor."

"It's *my* business. Nobody else's."

"Mine too," Lorelei firmly corrected her, "as long as I'm responsible. I know you have a good reason, Jenny, but you're a stranger to Mrs. Andrews. She thought it might be—almost anything."

Jenny felt her face stiffen, for Lorelei looked as if she expected something really awful. She couldn't let her think that. And there wasn't any way out. If she explained, it would cost Lorelei all that money. If she *didn't* explain, Horse might not get well. Unless . . . would Lorelei *possibly* go to the bank and help get her three hundred dollars?

"Lorelei—I know you have a lot of expenses!" she burst out. "That's the reason I want my money. *Please*, Lorelei, tell Mrs. Andrews I have to have it. It's my own—I've been saving it ever so long. And then you can buy your roof and paint and everything, and I can get a doctor for Horse."

Lorelei, who had been brushing back her bangs, stopped with her hand on her forehead. "Is *that* the reason you went to the bank!" she gasped.

"Yes. He has a terrible cough. Really a dreadful, awful one. And Pam said they had a horse with a cough like that, and it died. And his foot is sore. And he needs lots of grain. And—"

It was Lorelei's turn to interrupt. "Jenny," she said. "I didn't dream . . . I'm so busy that I don't pay as much attention to things around here as I should. But *why* didn't you tell me? *Why* did you go to a stranger?"

Now Jenny was the astonished one. "I just—I thought you didn't have enough money for a new roof and the plumbing leaks," she mumbled.

Lorelei shook her head. "Jenny, Jenny. Before you came, while we were planning your summer, your mother told me you're—well—independent. That you have a talent for getting into hot water. That I'd have to tie you down to get you to pay attention. But I really believed you'd talk things over with me." She made a wry face. "I guess I thought I was . . . well . . . younger. Approachable. That you and I would have a wonderful relationship. Only . . . apparently it isn't quite like that."

"I didn't mean to leave you out or anything" Jenny protested. "I just—I know paint and roofs and pipes cost a lot, so I didn't want you to spend your money." She drew a deep breath. "My mom thought a horse plus me would be too much for you, but I really wanted to come. I—well—I really kicked up quite a fuss. And I promised not to be a burden."

Lorelei was talking again. "Jenny, didn't you discuss expenses with your mother and father?"

Jenny shook her head.

"Of course the horse costs a lot. Your parents don't expect me to cover it—they sent plenty of money for him, along with your board." Lorelei was shaking her head. "I'm—I'm stunned, Jenny. I thought you knew. . . ."

Jenny screwed her eyes almost shut, trying to remember. They'd made the plans so fast, while her parents had been getting ready for their own trip. What had Mom been saying just before she boarded the plane? Something about not worrying and expenses, but she, Jenny, had only half listened, because it was all mixed up with the usual routine about try-to-be-a-help and be-sure-to-write-us-every-week. Maybe Mom was explaining about the money then. And Dad too. He'd said something, with his usual grin, about being behind her all the way. And for that matter, what had Lorelei said that first night? Arrangements? She hadn't really listened then, either, because she'd been trying not to show how terrible she felt.

Memories were flooding through Jenny's mind. Memories of the time she tried to teach herself ballet dancing, and fell and sprained her ankle. Of the time she signed up to ride Melody every Sunday, at the hour when it cost the least, and she'd forgotten it was church time, so she had to go back to Alec and tell him it wouldn't work. Of the time they went for a ski weekend and she told the instructor she knew how—and broke her shoulder. Of something her mother had said when they were talking about this summer: "*Please* don't go off on some harebrained scheme of your own."

"I'm sorry, Lorelei," she said. But she didn't feel as guilty as she knew she ought to, because a brand new, dazzling, exciting thought was crowding everything else right out of her head. Her parents had sent Lorelei enough money to get a doctor for Horse! To have him shod! To buy hay and grain, and even the high-pro mix! And it wouldn't interfere one speck with Lorelei's new roof.

Impulsively she jumped up and wrapped her cousin in a bear hug. "*Thank* you!" she exclaimed. "I know I should have told you all about it. Only . . ."

"We won't worry about that," Lorelei said, returning the hug. "It's water over the dam, and no real harm done. But—from here on—*please*, Jenny, cut me in on your problems."

"I will! Oh, yes, I will! Every time. And can we get the doctor right away? Tonight?"

Lorelei was smiling. "Well . . . it's pretty late now, but I'll have Mrs. Wilson call him the first thing tomorrow. We'll soon have that sad old friend of yours on the road to recovery."

"We'll get him shod? Fence the back lot?"

"That, too. Are you feeling better now?"

"I feel just wonderful!" Jenny replied. 'Thank you again! And Lorelei . . . Pam wants me to ride in the rodeo. If we get Horse in shape, maybe I can." She sat down again. "I'll be sure to tell you about *every little thing* ahead of time! Would that be all right? To enter it? Maybe I could win a ribbon."

"A great idea," Lorelei assured her. "We'll do it

for sure, if Horse gets well enough." She hesitated. "Of course, that may be a pretty big *if*. But we won't worry about it now." With another hug and a beaming smile, she went out the door.

So we'll get Horse—no, Farfalla—fixed up after all, thought Jenny as she snatched up her flashlight and raced down the path to the barn. He had water and a good thick bed of straw, but she gave him an extra measure of hay and rubbed his neck as he began to eat. He was coughing between bites, but she wouldn't think about that. Tomorrow the doctor would come. Farfalla would soon be well.

Returning to her room, she picked up her sketch pad and began to draw swiftly, placing the lines almost without thinking. When she was finished, she had drawn a picture of a long-legged horse, but it wasn't soaring over the jumps, as Cinnabar soared. It was wearing a Western saddle and making a tight turn around a barrel.

And this horse wasn't Cinnabar. It was dark—it was strong—it had stripes up its front legs, and its forehead star was shaped like a butterfly.

"A butterfly," Jenny murmured, giving him an extra-long tail. "Farfalla. We'll see what you can do."

7

What
the Doctor Said

*It is never wise to try to treat a sick animal
yourself. Only a veterinarian should make the
decision on which your horse's life may de-
pend.*

YOU AND YOUR EQUINE FRIEND, page 79.

"Jenny! Jenny! Lookit!"

"He's here, Jenny, in a big white truck!"

Hearing the shrill voices of Chip and Lissie, Jenny
ran out of the barn, where she had been perched disconsolately on the top board of Farfalla's stall. His
cough was worse today, as was his foot, and she had
been trying not to think of what Pam had said about
that other horse. *No matter what we did, he died.*

Maybe this horse would die! Maybe it was already
too late! And now, if Chip and Lissie were right, the
veterinarian had come at nine o'clock in the morning,
almost the very minute Mrs. Wilson called him. Had

he hurried because even on the telephone he could tell how sick Horse was?

Jenny ran through the barn door and up the path toward the house, just in time to see the white van come to a stop and the driver leap out, landing with a thump. Could *this* be a doctor? She had expected someone gray-haired and dignified in a sober business suit or perhaps a white jacket, but here was a towering, incredibly thin man with a curly black beard. Dressed in jeans, boots, and plaid shirt, he strode toward her, holding out his hand and smiling broadly, with a gleam of white teeth.

"Santoro! Dr. Santoro. But call me Mike," he announced in a growly voice, taking Jenny's hand in a firm grip and pumping it up and down. "I hear your horse is feeling poorly."

"He's really sick," she replied. She liked him already, this lanky, friendly, deep-voiced man. If anybody could save Horse, surely he was the one. "He's right here in the barn."

"Half a second." The doctor—Mike—returned to his van for a brown zippered bag. "My first line of defense," he explained, with another flashing smile, as he followed her into the barn, Chip and Lissie at his heels. He was so tall he had to duck his head when he went through the door.

They stopped beside the stall. "Hm-m-m," rumbled Mike. "Puny old fellow." As Horse shuffled toward them, he added, "Favors his leg. Coughing too, your mother told me."

"Not my mother . . . Mrs. Wilson. She takes care of the house while Lorelei—that's my cousin—is at work," Jenny hastily explained. "I'm visiting here for the summer."

"Well, let's have a look." The stall door squeaked as Mike swung it open. "I see you're keeping his quarters clean," he added. "That's one step in getting Friend, here, healthy."

Jenny felt her face turning pink with pride. She knew she ought to say a calm thank you, but it wouldn't come. "I . . . I tried," was the best she could manage.

"It's an awful lot of work," Chip broke in, looking up and up into Mike's face. "Sometimes we help. Me and Lissie."

"Good for you." Grinning, the doctor entered the stall. "You kids better stay outside. I know this old guy is your bosom buddy, but just the same, he might not appreciate my tender loving care." His voice dropped even deeper, and he pretended to frown. "He might even *kick*! So . . ." He turned serious. "So, let's be about it." Closing the stall door, he set his bag in the manger, while Lissie and Chip climbed onto their box in the adjoining stall and Jenny stood nearby.

"That's just like my doctor has," Lissie said in a stage whisper when Mike took out a stethoscope.

The doctor worked for some time in silence, listening to Farfalla's chest, taking his temperature, pry-

ing open his mouth to look at his throat with a flashlight, picking up each foot to check it. He spent
extra time with the left front one, and even though
he was gentle, Farfalla tried to jerk away. "Easy, old
fellow. Tender, isn't it?" he rumbled. With a final
pat on the bony chest, he jerked his head for Jenny
to follow, then led the way to the back porch.

"Now for a little chat," he began, doubling up his
long legs to sit on the third step. "There's something
I want to straighten out. You don't often see an animal in this condition. How long have you had him?"

"Just . . . well . . . four days, for me. Lorelei—
about two weeks. She bought this house, and when
she moved in—here he was."

"Ditched?" Mike stared. "Well—that's a new one!
Didn't the people who left him tell her where they
got him?"

"Not a word," said Jenny. "He was just here—
standing in the barn." She was beginning to panic.
Did he have to ask so many questions, as if they'd
stolen Horse? "Lorelei would have returned him if
she could. The Browns moved to Chicago, but she
telephoned them, and they don't want anything to
do with Horse. I mean Farfalla. They said he's ours.
So—"

"We found him, me and Lissie did!" Chip interrupted. "Mr. Brown told us there was a s'prise out
there, so we looked."

"And Mommie *really was* surprised," Lissie added.

"I'll bet." Mike grinned again. "So you haven't any history. Now—your Mrs. Wilson said the animal was very old. What's your guess?"

"Well . . . I—I'm not sure," Jenny stammered. "We think he's maybe twenty or even twenty-five."

Mike folded his bony arms and frowned. "What gave you that idea?"

"Mommie did. She says he's real old," Lissie volunteered. "But she didn't look at his teeth."

"Well, I did," said Mike, and a rumble of laughter welled up from deep within his chest. "I've heard some crazy stories, but this is the craziest one yet. Because, Jenny, he's a young horse. About seven years old."

"*Seven?*" Jenny stared. "You're sure?"

"Of course I'm sure. You can't miss it. In the prime of his life. I can't figure out why anyone would abandon him."

"But . . . he shuffles. . . ." Jenny stopped, remembering how nimbly Horse had run away to the hills.

"Neglect. He's half starved—you'll have to feed him well for a while. That'll make him your friend forever." Mike winked at her, then turned serious again. "He also has worms. About the worst case I've ever seen."

"Worms!" Jenny exclaimed.

"Right. No doubt about it. That accounts for at least part of his cough. Maybe all of it. You'll be surprised how fast he'll pick up, once he's rid of them. And he has an infection in his foot, which must be painful. Might have got started by stepping on a stone. When we get that cleaned up, and get rid of the worms and put some meat on his bones—say in two or three weeks—you'll think you have a different animal. But first I'll have to open the abscess and clean it up and give him some antibiotic."

"Can we watch?" asked Chip with instant interest. He had been standing with his hands clasped behind him, listening. "We'll be quiet," he hastened to add.

"As quiet as—as mice." This was Lissie.

Mike hesitated.

"Mommie let us watch when my rabbit had babies," Chip insisted, with a stubborn thrust of his chin, and then Mike said okay, he guessed it would be all right. "But you'll have to stay in the other stall. He can't kick you there."

"Will he kick you?" Chip asked.

Mike drew his black eyebrows together in a frown. "He'd *better not*! Tough, that's me." He spoke in a ferocious growl which made Lissie giggle.

Unfolding his long legs, Mike ambled over to his van and returned with another bag, larger than the first, and then led them all to the barn. There he fastened Farfalla's head with two straps, one to each side, which kept him from moving much in either direction.

"Cross-tie," he explained.

"I know," Jenny replied. "They tie horses that way at the Dexter, where I used to ride."

"Then you know all about it. Now, do you want

to get me some grain? To keep his mind off my fun and games."

"All I have is hay. I've bought some grain, but it hasn't come yet."

"Hay it is, then." Mike grinned again, while Jenny eagerly ran for a generous forkful and Chip and Lissie climbed back onto their box. Although the side between the two stalls was quite high, they could peer over the top board, with Jenny standing on the floor beside them.

Next Mike took out two enormous pills. "For worms. I'll give him the first dose today and another in a week." After putting the tablets, one at a time, into a device something like a huge syringe, he pried open Farfalla's mouth and placed them far back on his tongue, holding his mouth closed until he swallowed.

"Step number one. The next is harder." Mike moved his bag to the floor, close to the injured foot, and took out a square of plastic. "I'm going to open it, clean it up, and pack it with cotton and antibiotic."

"Hey! I can't *see*!" objected Chip, for Mike was crouched on the far side of Horse.

"Sorry, Sport," Mike replied. "This is the side the sore is on. You don't expect me to unhook his legs and switch them around, do you? Just to give you a ringside seat?"

" 'Course not," Chip stoutly replied, while Lissie hugged herself and giggled again.

"Will it hurt him?" she asked.

"Only a prick," Mike assured her. "About like

when the doctor gives you a shot. Actually, he'll feel better, soon as I let out the pus." He worked quietly for a few minutes, while Horse munched his hay. Once he jerked and snorted, and Mike rumbled, "Easy, boy."

Poor old guy, thought Jenny, as she watched. I wish he didn't have to be so sick and have his hoof cut open. It must feel awful.

A few minutes later Dr. Mike cheerfully announced, "All done." Grinning, he stood up and rubbed Farfalla on the nose. "Now that wasn't so bad, was it fellow?" He turned toward Jenny. "See —he's feeling better already, with some of that pressure relieved."

"May I ride him this weekend?"

"Well . . ." Mike scratched his beard. "Do you think you can wait a few days, until we get him out of the woods? Be better for him."

"I can wait," Jenny promised. She'd wait a long time, if that would get Farfalla well again.

Mike stayed a few more minutes, inquiring what kind of grain Jenny had bought and telling her how much to give him. A coffee can would do fine, he said, to measure it with. Then, after promising to return on Monday, he left, his van roaring down the lane until it was out of sight.

Half an hour later Pam arrived on Rocky, impatient to see what was wrong with Horse and how they had liked the doctor.

"He's *neat*!" She slid off Rocky's back and tied

him up, chattering as she worked. "Mike, I mean. I'm almost glad when we have a sick horse because then Mike comes, and he's so funny. He knows his business, too. My dad says so."

"You can see that all right," Jenny agreed. "Horse —Farfalla—is better already. And . . ." She caught her breath. "And Pam, he told us the most wonderful thing. Farfalla isn't old at all. He's *young*—only seven. When he's well, he'll be *lively*, and I can *really* ride." She repeated what Mike had said.

"Jenny!" Pam exclaimed. "It positively gives me goosebumps!" She ran into the barn with a carrot for Farfalla and patted his withers as she talked. "Just think—you had an old horse dumped on you, and now—he's young after all. So—we'll have some trail rides. Lots of them. By August you'll have him all trained, and can enter the rodeo with me. The barrel race."

"I'd love it," Jenny agreed. Today nothing bothered her, not even Pam's instant plans. She was going to have a young, strong horse, and he would be hers to ride all summer long. "But of course I don't know anything about rodeos, and probably Farfalla doesn't either."

"You'll learn. We'll work out in our corral."

"Maybe he'll win a prize. Only . . ." Jenny stopped. "Only if he wins, he might be worth a lot. Suppose he gets famous?"

Pam grinned, crinkling her red-brown eyes. "It's

actually not too likely. But if it did happen—what could be more thrilling than that?"

"It would be exciting all right," Jenny agreed, although she was troubled. Maybe, as Pam said, it wasn't likely. But it was possible. Horse—Farfalla—could be a winner, and if so . . . what next?

"Pam," she said, half ashamed, half determined. "Can we keep it sort of quiet—how I got Horse? I'm getting so I really like him, and I don't want somebody to come along and take him away from me."

Pam ran her hands through her flaming hair. "How could they do that, for Pete's sake?" she asked.

"Well, if they knew he just got left in Lorelei's barn, they might say he was theirs. That somebody stole him."

Pam's eyes opened wide. "They might, at that."

"He really is mine!" Jenny argued. "If I hadn't come, he'd be dog food by now. So . . ."

"So—okay—we won't say anything about it. No use stirring up trouble."

Later that afternoon, shortly after Pam had left for home, Jenny's order from the feed store arrived, and she happily told the delivery man where to put it—hay and straw in two piles in the feed room, both kinds of grain on the shelf, and salt block at the end of Falla's manger.

And now—happy thought—to feed him! How much grain had Mike told her to start with? Two coffee-cans full, she thought. Or was it three? Deciding to be conservative and stick to two, she used the coffee can Lorelei had given her, measured out the exact amount, and watched eagerly while Horse devoured every morsel and sniffed in the corners for more.

"You *love* it!" she exclaimed as she brought him a bucket of fresh water. "It must be ages since you've had anything half that good."

She decided not to let him graze. "Got to keep you quiet," she said, brushing his coat for the second time that day. Farfalla snuffled with contentment and closed his eyes, rubbing his muzzle against her arm. "Really, you're a nice old guy—no, that's not right. A nice *young* guy," she told him.

After dinner she returned to the stall. "Hay all gone, too? Well you poor starving fellow, we'll just give you a little something to sleep on," she murmured. It had been at least an hour since his other meal—surely he could have some more by now—but not too much, of course. Humming softly, she poured almost another canful of grain, added some hay, and since his water was gone, she refilled the bucket. "There—that ought to hold you for the night," she said, and after planting one last kiss on his forehead, she ran up the path to the house.

By nine o'clock she was yawning. "I think I'll go to bed," she told Lorelei, who had sorted a box of children's clothes and was ready to work on her book. " 'Night, now."

" 'Night."

Lulled by the faint tapping of the typewriter, Jenny fell almost at once into a deep, dreamless sleep. But later on—she couldn't even guess how much later—something awakened her, and she ran to the window listening. There it was again, not loud, but quite clear in the still air. Something was making a deep, low sound, something in the direction of the barn. It was a sound she had never heard before.

Throwing on a robe and sneakers and picking up her flashlight, Jenny ran swiftly down the stairs and out the door. It was quite cold outside, and a full moon cast dense black shadows under the trees. Out here in the open the sounds were much louder, as if someone were moaning in pain. Tense with fear, she ran as fast as she could down the lane, flung open the barn door, and turned her flashlight onto Falla's stall.

He was there, and he was alone. But when she saw him, she caught her breath, for he was stretched out on his side in the straw, jerking his legs and twisting his head in order to bite at his stomach.

And he was groaning. Even though Jenny had little experience with ailments of horses, she could see at a glance that this one was serious. Farfalla was really sick.

8

++

In the Night

*The best way to make friends with your horse
is to care for it yourself. This will sometimes
require sacrifices on your part.*

YOU AND YOUR EQUINE FRIEND, page 58.

"Falla!" Jenny exclaimed, dropping to her
knees beside him. "What's wrong?" Not seeming to
realize she was there, he let out another deep moan.

"Falla—*Falla!*" Jenny felt his head, his throat, his
side. "What's *happened*?" He moaned again, lifted
his head, and let it fall with a thud to the straw.

Dr. Mike! Jenny thought. *I've got to get him fast.*
She flew up the path to the house, slipped quietly into
the front hall, and dialed his number as softly as she
could, so she wouldn't waken Lorelei.

The doctor was at home, and when Jenny, almost
in a whisper, told him about Horse, he rumbled,

"Think I'd better have a look. Get him up, if you can, and I'll be right over."

Get him up! Jenny thought. How can I get a big thing like a horse to stand up if he doesn't want to? Laying down the telephone, she raced upstairs to dive into jeans and a sweater, then returned to the barn.

There she took hold of horse's neck and lifted. Pulled on the halter straps. Got in back and pushed. Nothing worked. Farfalla lay flat, groaning, still twisting his head sidewise to bite at his side. "You act as if you had a stomach ache," Jenny told him. "And it must be a terrible, awful one, from the way you sound." She thought he was swollen—unless she didn't know how a horse was supposed to look lying down.

While she was still struggling, a bright light suddenly shone on them, and Dr. Mike came into the barn, carrying a gasoline lantern. He didn't enter the stall, but gave the horse one quick glance. "Colic," he said, grim behind his beard. "Bad case, I'd say. Jenny, you'd better get your cousin."

"I don't want to wake her up," Jenny told him. "Please."

"Hm-m. I need a helper."

"I'll help you. He's mine—sort of—I know lots more about horses than Lorelei does. And I'm already awake. So, please, let Lorelei sleep."

Dr. Mike scratched his head. "Tough cookie, are you?"

"*Very* tough," Jenny replied, at which the doctor almost smiled. "All right. We'll give Lorelei her beauty rest, at least for a while. Just you and me and the horse."

He strode out of the barn, returning at once with a plastic jug filled with liquid and the same large bag he had carried earlier. "I need a clean bucket," he crisply said, and Jenny ran to wash one they had used for the bath.

"Good," he said when she returned. He already had a hypodermic syringe ready to use. "First, a shot to cut his pain. Make him easier to manage. He won't mind it." He thrust in the needle, and in a moment drew it out.

"Step one," he said. "Now let's see if we can get him up. You squat down behind and push, while I pull on the halter."

Jenny did as Mike said. Although at first Falla lay flat, he finally, with many groans, poked out his front feet, lurched upward—and, with Mike still tugging on the rope, came upright. He was shaking; his sides were wet with sweat; he continually twisted his head around to bump his nose against his stomach.

"Good," Mike said. "Now, Jenny, take hold of this rope. When I tell you, pull it high and tight so he has to hold his head up. Use all the muscle you have. Luckily he's a docile animal. I'll be ready in a minute."

Working fast, he poured the contents of the jug into the bucket. "Mineral oil," he briefly said in reply to Jenny's question. "A gallon." He took a long coiled tube out of his bag. "Ready now, Jenny. Hold him up."

He helped her raise Falla's head, and then she kept it high while he threaded the tube up the animal's nose. "All the way into his stomach," he said. "He'd fight it, only he's too sick to care. It doesn't hurt him. Just not very comfortable."

Inch by inch the tube slid up the nose, until Mike said it had gone far enough, fastened a funnel onto the end, held it high, and started to pour the oil. It gurgled, and Horse jerked his head. "Steady!" Mike advised. "Hang in there." So Jenny braced her feet and lifted on the halter with all her strength, keeping Falla's head as still as she could until all the oil was gone.

"Such a lot!" she gasped when Mike with withdrawing the tube.

"A horse is a lot of animal," he replied with a faint grin.

While he was repacking his equipment, he gave her directions. "The first thing he'll try to do is lie down again, and we can't have that. So, somebody's got to stay with him all night and keep him on his feet. He mustn't go down."

"I'll do it," Jenny promptly said.

Mike shook his head. "Too big a job for you, Jenny. It's going to be a long time. Four hours—five. What time is it now?"

"Two—almost half-past," said Jenny, glancing at

her watch. "I couldn't sleep anyway. Besides, Falla is really my job. Lorelei doesn't know anything about a horse."

Dr. Mike grinned. "Nope. No way I'm going off and leave you here by yourself. So go get your cousin, and I'll put her in charge." Jenny couldn't persuade him to change his mind.

Lorelei awoke instantly when Jenny touched her shoulder. "Sick? Falla?" she said, sleep still in her voice. "What happened?"

"I'm not sure," Jenny replied. "But Dr. Mike is about ready to leave, and he says you have to know about it."

"All right. I'll come." Lorelei swung her feet to the floor and picked up her robe.

Outside, where Mike was leading Falla back and forth beside the barn, he quickly explained what had happened. "Colic. It means somebody has to keep him moving, probably all the rest of the night."

"I can do that," Jenny insisted. "*Please*! If it's too hard, I'll call you, Lorelei, but you go back to bed now. You have to work tomorrow, but I can sleep then, if Falla's all right."

"I actually think Jenny can handle it," Dr. Mike agreed, walking Falla in a small circle. "He's a nice, docile animal, and she has quite a way with him. The only reason I had her call you was because I didn't want to leave her alone without cuing you in. But if you know how the land lies, and can help her if she has trouble—that's all we need."

"Suppose he gets worse?"

"I don't think he will. Luckily we caught it early, and a good dose of mineral oil generally gives relief in a few hours. It isn't too much for Jenny, provided you know what's up and will lend a hand if she needs it."

"*Please!*" Jenny said again, and Lorelei at last consented. "Provided you call me if you have any trouble. But first—run upstairs and put on more clothes. It's cold out here." Shivering, she returned to bed.

"Now," said the doctor when Jenny came back, bundled to the eyebrows. "Do you know what to do?"

"Just—keep him walking. Call Lorelei if he lies down and I can't get him up. And if she and I both can't do it, we'll telephone you."

"Right. I don't think you'll have any trouble," Mike told her. "But it's going to be a long night."

"I know it. If he gets cold, shall I put him into the stall?"

"No—you may get cold, but he won't. Take him up and down the lane, because the footing is good there, and it's dark. Use your flashlight, if you want to—there's a moon, which will help some. Just keep him moving."

"I will," Jenny promised. "I won't stop for a single minute."

"Incidentally," Mike said, frowning. "Your horse must have had something to eat that set this off. Apples? Potatoes?"

"Nothing like that," Jenny assured him. "Just his regular food. It came this afternoon."

Mike stopped walking. "Did you follow my directions?"

"I think so. I only gave him some grain. And a drink."

"How much?"

"Two cans—like you said. I was really careful," Jenny told him. "He liked it so much that before I went to bed I fed him again."

"How much?"

"Just a little. Not even a whole canful." She stared earnestly at the doctor. "The first meal didn't last him at all, and he was so hungry, and he'd been having such an awful time with his foot. I wanted him to have something good to sleep on." She stopped, for Dr. Mike—nice, kind, jolly Dr. Mike—looked so serious.

"Two cans, plus a little. That shouldn't have kicked up all this. Unless . . ." He snapped his finger. "Jenny —show me the can."

She ran to fetch it.

"I thought so. Jenny, this is a three-pound can. You ought to use the smaller ones—one-pounders—to measure with. I think I told you that."

Jenny suddenly remembered. "I think so, too," she mumbled, looking down.

"So instead of giving him two pounds, you gave him—seven? Eight? No wonder he had trouble. In the future, Jenny, remember that horses are dingbats about food. They'll eat their heads off if you let them."

Jenny was ready to cry. "You mean—I made him sick?"

"Well—let's just say the feed did. You'll get it straight after this." Mike picked up his bag and handed over the lead rope. "Here, I'll help with the first trip down the lane, and then it's all up to you."

Together they led Horse outside and walked him slowly toward the house. "Keep him going, but don't rush him," Mike advised. "If he tries to lie down, lift on the rope so his head is high. And if you can't do it, even with Lorelei to help you, be sure to give me another call. Colic can be fatal—it's nothing to fool with." With a rattle and crunch his truck was gone, leaving Jenny with Horse.

It was an eerie feeling to be alone in the dark, walking up and down the lane, while the pale moon sank in the west. Horse still groaned as he shuffled slowly along, toward the house, away from the house, with Jenny humming softly, or talking to him.

"Good fellow," she murmured over and over, stroking his shaggy neck. "It's awful, but you'll be better soon."

Horse groaned again, stumbled, almost fell, and although Jenny pulled with all her strength, he planted his feet, unwilling to move.

"Come on now, there's a good horse," she coaxed. "Have to keep moving." At last, with a heavy sigh, he lumbered on.

Shadows lay black, the wind was blowing, and before long Jenny was cold in spite of her heavy clothes. "But I can't leave you," she told him. "If I do, you might lie down. Maybe you can get me warm." She stopped walking for a few moments and put both hands on his furry neck, while Horse laid his long head on her shoulder and breathed in her ear. "You're a nice old thing," she said. "I think you know I'm trying to help." He groaned again, letting his head rest on her still more heavily.

Crunch—crunch. Their footsteps sounded together. The moon sank, leaving the lane so dark that Jenny turned on her flashlight. Twice Farfalla blew out a mighty sigh and almost sank to the ground, but Jenny frantically jerked on his head, pulling and pulling as high as she could, until he groaned and started to walk again.

Jenny felt as if she had lead in her shoes. "Please, Horse—no, Falla—get well," she said. Trying to stay awake, she sang to herself in a thin little voice, new songs and old songs and songs she made up as she went along. She mustn't let herself fall asleep, not now, so she stumbled on beside Falla, back and forth, back and forth, with one hand holding the rope and the other clutching his mane. When the sky turned light, she didn't realize it, and when Lorelei came outside, she was still plodding along, leaning against Falla with her eyes shut.

"Jenny!" Lorelei cried. "You're out on your feet. Why didn't you call me?"

"I'm f-fine," Jenny mumbled.

"Well, you need some rest. I'll call Dr. Mike this minute and have him come take a look at Horse. And in the meantime, I'll do the walking." Lorelei hurried away, returning almost at once.

"I reached him," she said. "He'll be right over."

"Okay. But I'm going to stay in the barn," Jenny replied.

Lorelei brought her a blanket so she could curl up on a bench in the tack room, where she fell asleep at once. Even in her dream she thought she was still walking Horse, back and forth, back and forth in the dark.

Later on she awoke to find Dr. Mike standing beside her and whistling a cheerful tune.

"You've done a good job," he said. "Your friend will be all right now. Just don't be quite so generous next time."

"I'll be sure," she promised him eagerly, and as soon as Mike had gone, she stumbled upstairs to throw herself into bed.

The long night was behind her at last. She'd never forget how patiently the horse had shuffled along beside her, or his groans, or his warm sides when she laid her icy hands against them. She'd never forget how sick he had been.

But now—Farfalla was going to get well.

9

Riding

Your job as handler would be easier if your horse could talk. Since that is impossible, you must learn to "read" sign language. Every action—pricking the ears, laying them back, snorting, breathing hard—all of these tell you how the animal feels.

YOU AND YOUR EQUINE FRIEND, page 137.

Early Monday morning Mike returned to change the dressing on Falla's foot and give him more antibiotic. "Infection going down," he said, looking pleased. "That's the way we want it." He grinned at Jenny and rumbled, "No, young lady. No riding yet. But you can lead him outside, at a walk, for a little while every day."

"He's so much better," Jenny said. "He's hardly limping at all. And we're having his yard fenced, so he won't have to be tied."

116

"Good. Every horse deserves his own pasture."

The fence was in place when Dr. Mike came again on Thursday, and he beamed as he fed Horse a carrot. "Everything under control." Farfalla nosed his pocket. "I see he's acquiring some spirit, too. Any problems? Tractable?"

"No problems. He acts as if he likes us, and he's a lot less bony already."

"Right. You've waited a long time." Whistling a tuneless little whistle, Mike carefully re-packed his bag. "It's almost time for a ride at last. Not too long, and no running. But first call the farrier, and have him shod. See . . . his hoofs are cracked and split, and much too long. Let's say you have him shod Monday and go for a ride—not too far—the next day. Can you remember to take it easy for another week?"

"I'll be careful . . . oh, I will," Jenny promised. She felt as if she would shake her hand off, waving, when Mike drove away in his white van.

Except for being unable to ride Farfalla, the weekend was fun. They all dug into the job of settling and worked on something every day: a few boxes, a cupboard, a closet. Busy as they were, they still had time to go to a ball game and take a picnic into the hills. And then it was the new week.

Before any one else was up on Monday morning, Jenny rushed to the barn. She'd noticed how dusty the saddle blanket was, and she wanted everything just right for her first real ride, so she carried it to the basement, sudsed and rinsed it in the old-fashioned laundry tubs, then hung it outside on the fence to dry. Hardly tasting her breakfast, she hummed along with Lissie. Farfalla was better. Today he was going to be shod.

Just after Lorelei left, the farrier's black pickup truck rattled down the lane, so Jenny abandoned the rest of her oatmeal and dashed out the door. Lissie and Chip followed close behind, each munching a sticky piece of toast and jam.

"Hamilton Knox." The man seized Jenny's hand in his, hard as a block of wood, with a grip so tight she winced. "Folks call me Ham." He was a wiry, little bow-legged man with a huge, bawling voice, all out of proportion to his size. "Horse still in his stall? Well, get him out," he roared. "Right there, by the barn, is where we'll work." He backed his truck into place, while Jenny led Farfalla outside and tied him to one of the rings.

Ham's truck held racks of tools, boxes of horse-shoes, and a small forge, which he clamped onto the tailgate. Shouting to Jenny, shouting answers to Chip's questions, he selected an enormous pair of clippers, then approached Farfalla.

"Really is a big one," he bellowed. "*Git* over, there. *Git* over." This was to the horse, while he nudged him into place and lifted a front foot. "You called me just in time. This here's really overgrown." Anchoring the foot between his knees and manipu-lating the clippers with two hands, he trimmed the hoof and filed it smooth. "Cracks like this might cause a peck of trouble."

"Does that hurt him?" asked Lissie, wide-eyed.

"Does it hurt to trim your fingernails?" boomed Ham.

"Course not," she replied, with a giggle.

"Well then—same idea."

With the hoofs trimmed, Ham lighted his forge and hammered the shoes into shape, trying each for size, returning it to the flame and pounding some more. Last of all he nailed the shoes in place, and when he was through, Farfalla stood with his feet close together, neat and proud, as if he were pointing his toes.

"He looks so *pretty*! Like a ballet dancer," Jenny said.

"Right you are," Ham agreed. "Horses need their feet tended, same as folks. Oil his hoofs every day now, and I'll be back in six weeks." He slid the forge into its rack.

"Six weeks? Will he need new shoes so soon?" Jenny asked in surprise.

"Prob'ly not. But he'll need a trim. Prob'ly can use the same shoes again. But them hoofs are so over-grown they'll have to be cut back in easy stages." With a final pat for Farfalla and wink for Lissie and Chip, Ham was gone.

Jenny raced to telephone Pam, then returned to her horse. Dr. Mike had said she could ride him tomorrow—but surely one day wouldn't matter. Not if she didn't go far, and she positively couldn't wait another minute.

Since the saddle blanket was still wet, she brought out one of the others, along with the saddle and bridle. Fumbling in her eagerness, getting the straps all wrong and having to do them over, but eventually managing to cinch everything tight, she put them on. "Now, Falla," she said, with a catch in her throat. "Here we are. Ready at last."

She swung into the saddle. But before she had her feet in the stirrups, Farfalla snorted, arched his back, and jumped up and down with his knees stiff, promptly throwing her off.

"Farfalla!" she indignantly yelled, standing up and brushing the dust off her jeans, while the children scrambled to the safety of the back steps. "You *bad horse*! You've been *babied*, that's what!"

He watched her warily, ears laid back and nostrils flaring, and when she walked toward him, he backed away. But thanks to the new fence he couldn't run far, so she quickly caught him again.

"He still doesn't feel good," Lissie called.

"He's just spoiled," Jenny called back. "We can't let him get away with it." Gritting her teeth, she again swung into the saddle.

This time she managed to stay on for three wrenching jolts, then found herself, as before, sprawled on the ground.

Pam's coming, she thought. She'll know what to

do. Jumping up, she folded her arms and cautiously eyed Farfalla, who was still breathing hard with his ears back. "I don't think you're a bad horse," she said, reaching for the reins. She had left the rope fastened to the ring in the barn wall, so she tied him there. "You look almost scared. We'll wait a while and try again."

A few minutes later, when Pam rode Rocky down the lane, Jenny told her all in a breath what had happened.

"Wow!" Pam said, sliding to the ground, her eyes bright with excitement. "Let's have a look. Horses don't act like that for nothing." She approached Farfalla softly, clucking her tongue. "You saddled him? Have you done that by yourself before?"

"Yes, at the Dexter. I think I got it right."

"Hm-m. The girth's okay. Let's look underneath."

She unfastened the strap, lifted off the saddle, and slid her hand under the blanket, then threw back her head in a burst of laughter. "Wow! Of *course* he bucked! You've got some chaparral under there! Didn't you *look*? Even our old Daisy Mae would have fits if we did that."

Rolling her eyes, she pulled out a twisted black stem, not very long, but armed with thorns. "See? How'd you like to have that grinding into your back? With somebody on top?"

"Pam! Poor old guy! And I called him a bad horse!"

"Just let it be a lesson to you," Pam said, as she vigorously shook the blanket, then replaced it and put on the saddle. "Even a clean blanket isn't safe, and this looks as if it's hung around practically forever."

"I won't forget again," Jenny promised, with a miserable glance at Farfalla, who had stopped trembling and was breathing calmly. "Good boy . . . steady there," she crooned and cautiously mounted. At last, at last, she was ready to start.

Pam on Rocky led the way along the street to the end of the block, where she turned away from town onto a two-track jeep road. It led across a broad valley with mountains all around, and now Jenny found that the land wasn't flat, as she had thought, but quite rough, with gouged-out gullies and enormous outcroppings of stern gray rock. Sagebrush stood in silver-gray bunches; mesquite lifted its twisted black stems; flowers grew everywhere—daisies, flame-colored Indian paint brush, tiny blue and yellow ones whose names she didn't know.

"That's the old trail," Pam said as they passed a narrow path that branched off to the right. "It's a short cut to Pinnacle Rock—the biggest rock around. You'll see it pretty soon. But since they built this jeep road, hardly anybody uses the old one because it's so steep."

In a few minutes they came to a barbed wire fence, with the wide bars of a cattle guard in the roadbed. Vehicles with wheels could cross this, but animals' hoofs might slip through, so they had to follow the narrow path beside it, through a wire gate.

"Everything beyond here is open range," Pam said

as she pulled a loop of wire off a post and held back a section of fence to let the horses pass. "It's national forest. Miles and miles, with lots of cattle, but nothing else, and pretty soon, up in the mountains, you're in the Bridger Wilderness."

"It's so—so big," Jenny replied with a shudder. She was thinking how tame her trail rides at home had been, close to town and always with a leader.

"We'd better start back," she said before they had gone far. "It's Falla's first real ride, and I don't want him to get too tired. Actually, I was supposed to wait until tomorrow."

"Right," Pam replied. "We'll go exploring some other time." Pulling Rocky to a halt, she pointed toward the white-capped mountains that loomed against the horizon, higher and farther than the foothills. "Some day we'll ride up there. That's the Wind River Range, and that highest one, with the most snow, is called The Old Man. You can see him from town, if you know where to look."

"It makes me feel—really small," Jenny replied.

That was the first of many days when Jenny rode, alone or with Pam, through the valleys and hills. Sometimes she went high into the wilderness, where towering trees stood beside clear blue lakes. Sometimes she explored the valley. Every morning, as she had promised, she gave Lissie and Chip a ride.

Nourished by hay and grain, Falla began to lose his bony look, to pick up his feet, and to prick his ears. His cough and limp were gone. His coat began to shine, almost black in the shade, glistening brown in the sun.

To the girls' surprise, he had been well trained. "By somebody kind," Pam said. "Or he wouldn't be so well-mannered."

Sometimes they rode with other girls, friends of Pam's, most of whom were going to be in the barrel races at the county rodeo.

"Racing is *fun*!" a slim little dark-eyed girl said. "You ought to try it." She rode a paint, brown and white.

"I will, if Falla's well enough," Jenny promised. "But I don't know how."

"It mostly depends on the turns. Unless they're good and tight you lose a lot of time."

"Just so you don't knock over a barrel," added a big, hearty girl, who had just ridden up on a gray gelding. "They penalize you for that, and it ruins your chances."

It was fun to be making friends, fun to compare horses and talk about training them, or compare notes on the best saddle soap or hoof oil. But Jenny never discussed Falla's past.

"My cousin's horse," she said when anyone asked her. "Actually I'm not sure where he's from, but I'm hoping to take him home with me in the fall." I ought to want to find his real owner, she thought. But Falla's mine! I saved him twice. From being dog food. From dying of colic.

Although their first rides were short, they gradually increased them until mid-July, when Jenny had been riding for three weeks. It was time to start training for the rodeo, they decided, so early on a Monday morning Jenny rode to the ranch and found Pam in the corral.

"Jenny!" She trotted Rocky to the fence. "Here at last! We'll get right at it. See—my Dad has the barrels already in place." She paused, with a grin. "We've got an audience, too." Her father was leaning against the corral fence beside two cowhands who were perched on the top rail.

"Up and at it!" one of them called, waving his broad-brimmed hat.

Pam's father strode forward to open the gate. He was a big man with flaming red hair like Pam's and the same crinkly slit of his eyes when he grinned. "Hi, Jenny," he said. "Pam's told me about your horse, but I expected a pitiful specimen, not this handsome fellow."

"He *was* pitiful," Jenny said, with a smile.

"Well . . . he looks great now." As he walked all around Falla, feeling his haunches, his flanks, his legs, Jenny grew uneasy. Why was he so interested? But in a few minutes he gave Falla a brisk slap on the rump and grinned. "Must be part thoroughbred. Not a quarter horse or Morgan, that's for sure, and big as he is, he may have trouble with the turns."

"I know it. But I want to try."

"Good girl. Let's see what he can do." Mr. Winokur returned to the corral fence.

Before starting, Pam and Jenny let the horses sniff the barrels—empty oil barrels, painted white—while Pam explained that some of the turns were clockwise and some counter-clockwise, which meant reversing the direction of the turn.

"Watch me," she said and took Rocky to the starting point.

At first Jenny thought she would never get the hang of it because she kept going the wrong way around and making the turns too wide.

"Jenny!" Pam exclaimed after the first few attempts. "*What* are you doing? This is a *race!*"

"I don't want him to run into a barrel."

"He'll clear them all right. Give him credit for a *little* sense!" Pam clucked her tongue and started Rocky off. "Watch!" He turned in a scuffle of dust, pivoting on his back legs, missing the barrels by inches. "Now try again. When you're ready to turn right, lay your reins that way and kick with your left foot. Turning left—just the opposite. You have to do it at the very best instant. Steer him close, and let him do the dodging."

"Okay," Jenny agreed and started Farfalla again.

She worked for nearly an hour that afternoon, the next, and the next, soon learning which way to go, and the exact fraction of a second to give Falla the all-important kick. Some days she and Pam rode alone; sometimes they were joined by the other girls. And gradually Farfalla improved.

"I think that was better," she called one day after an unusually swift run. "He lurched more, sort of a spin."

"He's plenty fast on the straightaway," Pam agreed. "It's only his turns."

"*Only* the turns!" Jenny exclaimed. "The most important part." To Farfalla she added more softly, "You get an extra apple today for trying so hard."

The days slipped by. Every morning Jenny brushed Farfalla and cleaned his stall, gave the children their ride, then rode him to the ranch for practice with the barrels. The rodeo was three weeks away—two—one.

One hot day of the last week, after coming home and taking care of Farfalla, she wearily climbed the stairs, ready to curl up with a book. However, Chip's door was closed, and she heard muffled sounds from inside. Something's wrong, she thought, as she knocked and heard a soft, "Come in."

She found Chip face down on the bed, with Lissie beside him, humming a sad little tune. Honey was perched on the headboard, squawking from time to time.

"It's his pollywogs," Lissie whispered. "He left Honey loose, and he got in here and killed them all." The goldfish bowl, precariously cradled in the crook of Chip's elbow, held only a few limp black scraps.

Jenny sat down on the bed. Ferocious bird, with its cruel beak and glittering eyes. Maybe she could help.

"Something like this always happens to pollywogs, Chip," she said softly. "Mine died, too. All but one, and I let him go in the lagoon."

"But Honey. . . ." Chip's voice was thick with tears. "Honey shouldn't have *done* it." He buried his face again, bursting into fresh sobs. "He's supposed to be *nice!*"

Jenny knew Chip was mourning as much for Honey as the tadpoles. He's only five, she thought, and it's hard to find out that somebody you love— even a bird—doesn't measure up.

"Chip," she said, stroking the back of his neck. "This doesn't mean Honey is bad. He's a bird, and wild birds have to eat little moving creatures in order to live. Honey was being good . . . by a bird's rules."

Chip continued to sob.

"I've an idea," Jenny continued. "We could have a funeral. With you and Lissie as chief mourners."

Half turning over and slopping water out of the bowl, Chip cocked one eye at her.

"I could sing," Lissie volunteered. "I know some really sad songs."

At this Chip sat up. "Do you think we can find a little box?"

"Mommie saves boxes on our present-wrapping shelf," Lissie suggested. "I'll get one." Humming a mournful tune, she clumped downstairs and in five minutes was back with a small box in which she tenderly arranged the tadpoles.

"This will be a swell funeral," Chip exclaimed.

"First my robot can carry them." He put the box in the hook-like hands, said, "Go—Go Boy," and watched the metal man lurch across the floor.

"Now we'll give them a ride on the train." Putting the box on the flat-car, he ran it twice around the track.

"And now we'll dig a grave." While Lissie sang an appropriately sad song, he took the box downstairs for burial under a cottonwood tree.

By then Chip was deep in plans for catching more tadpoles. "I know 'zactly where. The same pond where I got these, and there were lots all around the edge."

"Next year," Jenny suggested. "This late in summer they'll be almost frogs, away out in the pond, and hard to catch."

"No!" Chip insisted, squaring his chin. "*This* year. These are bullfrog tadpoles, and they live a long time. Mommie helped me look them up in our nature book. I know we can get some. You could take me on Falla."

"Well—we'll see."

"If he says this year, he means this year," Lissie advised in a stage whisper. "Mommie says he's like a runaway locomotive. When he gets started down the wrong track, nothing can stop him."

Jenny sighed. "Chip, I'm not going to make any promises I can't keep. I don't know whether you can find tadpoles this late in summer, and I don't know *when* I'll take you. This week I'm saving Farfalla for the rodeo. But some time—remember, I'm just saying *some time*—when the rodeo is over—if your mother agrees—I'll take you to the pond, and you can try."

In an instant Chip was all smiles. "Promise?" he demanded, blue eyes sparkling.

"I promise. When Falla's through with his race."

"C'mon, Lissie. Let's go over to Tim and Terry's house." Chip flung his arms around Jenny's neck, gave her a sticky kiss, and was gone.

For those last few days Jenny gave Falla only a light workout, and on Friday she let him spend most of his time in the back lot. At mid-afternoon she ran outside to the barn.

"Not a full bath," she told him. "You're already pretty clean, and besides, you might take cold. We'll just shine you up a bit." Humming under her breath, she collected two buckets of warm water, a sponge, and a bottle of her best shampoo. "Just your mane and tail and legs," she said as she tied him beside the barn in the sun. "If you're patient, you'll soon have a nice can of grain."

She scrubbed his legs, brushed out the mane and tail, poured on shampoo. "Lissie is right," she said as she rinsed off the suds. "A horse is very big. But I'll oil your hoofs—and we're through."

Kneeling beside Falla's left front leg and shoving against him until he shifted his weight, she picked up his foot. "Oh, oh—a pebble!" she exclaimed as she dug it out. "Can't have you going lame on the big day!" One by one she went over the hoofs until they were all clean and oiled, then put Farfalla back into his stall, fed him, and gave him fresh water. Leaning his head against her shoulder, he heaved a big sigh of contentment.

She had done everything she could. Tomorrow was the rodeo, and Farfalla's chance—her chance, too—to show what they could do.

10

‡‡

Rodeo

In western riding the reins are slack, giving the horse freedom to use its head in maintaining balance. This permits quick stops, starts and turns. It also requires you to give commands by neck reining, shifting your weight, and nudging with your heels.

YOU AND YOUR EQUINE FRIEND, page 177.

The next morning Jenny bounded out of bed the instant she awoke. She had to oil Falla's hoofs again, make sure he had enough to eat, but not too much, and ride him to the rodeo grounds. She had a lot to do.

Breakfast was hectic because Lissie and Chip chattered and spilled things and bounced in their chairs. "Do you think Falla will *win*?" demanded Chip with his mouth full.

"He might. But I don't really think so," Jenny replied as calmly as she could when her heart was thumping. "He isn't as fast as Rocky."

"But he still *could* win!"

"Well—maybe."

"Win or lose, we'll be rooting for you," Lorelei said with a smile. "Chip—not at the table." Chip had Honey perched on his shoulder and was feeding him oatmeal.

"Ah-oh," squawked Honey as Chip stood up to put him away.

"He's mad," Chip explained. "He wants to play. But he can't because we won't be here." Returning to his chair, he scooped oatmeal around and around his bowl. "Mommie—can we go right now? I'm not hungry."

"And we *have* to get there early," Lissie urged. "We don't want to miss Jenny's race, do we?"

"No need to worry about that, when Jenny hasn't even left yet," Lorelei told them, laughing. "Now, let's all get busy and clear up the dishes while she takes care of Falla."

"*Thank* you, Lorelei," Jenny exclaimed, giving her an impulsive hug. She snatched up her jacket and ran down the path to the barn.

Farfalla was watching calmly over the top of his stall, and when she slipped in beside him, he sighed and leaned his head against her arm. "Nice old thing," she murmured, stroking his long, bristly face. "Little do you guess what excitement you're going to have today." He nosed her pockets. "Looking for a carrot?

Well, here you are. Only it's last night's apple core."
Unwrapping a soggy brown morsel, she held it on the
flat of her hand and giggled at the tickly touch of
his lips.

And now she must hurry. This is our big day, she
thought, as she brought Falla food and water, checked
and oiled his hoofs, and brushed out his mane and
tail.

Ten minutes later she was on the black-top road to
the County Fair Grounds, jogging along the shoulder
because it was softer than the pavement, and safer
from the cars and horse trucks that were streaming
by. Early as it was, a hot sun blazed in the intensely
blue sky. A pheasant squawked and ran across the
road; a jack-rabbit bounded over a field.

As Jenny neared the entrance to the performer's
area, she heard the loudspeaker playing country mu-
sic, and through a gap in the bleachers she saw a tank-
truck in the main arena sprinkling down the dust.
"How soon will it begin?" she asked the official at the
gate, giving him her name.

"Oh—'bout fifteen minutes," he answered with a
grin. "They're lining up for the parade now. That's
a mighty handsome animal you've got there. Going
to barrel-race him?"

"I'm hoping to," Jenny replied, trying to smile.

"Well—good luck. You'll find a whole covey of
girls back there, nervous as cats."

As Jenny rode across the outer arena, she heard a

voice singing over the speaker. "You are my sunshine, my only sunshine." One stall was selling cokes and hot dogs, another had bandanas and broad-brimmed hats, and a red-faced man was hawking silver jewelry. At the farthest edge stood a large van labeled PRICE'S DOG FOOD—THE BEST FOR LESS. "You might have gone there, if I hadn't come along," she told her horse, who waggled his ears. "That makes you really mine."

Jenny passed groups of riders bunched close together, struggling to keep their horses quiet. Where's Pam? she thought. I promised to meet her here. Just as she decided she'd have to find her own way around, she spotted Rocky.

"I almost gave you up," shouted Pam, pale under her freckles.

"No matter. Nothing's started yet. But Jenny, you look so hot! Red as a beet!"

"I am hot, and so is Falla. I've got to give him a drink." Jenny slid off his back and started to smooth his coat with the brush she had brought in her shirt pocket.

"Okay. But not too much. He can't run if he's waterlogged." Pam showed Jenny a faucet and bucket, then led her toward the other barrel riders. "There's an awful racket, but Falla's got to get used to it. Will he shy?"

"He might. He's jittery already."

"Well, keep talking. Right into his ear."

Today I don't care how much she bosses me around, Jenny thought as she rode slowly along. *I need all the help I can get.*

At the far end of the staging area a group of teen-age girls were gathered on their horses, some of which were standing quietly, others tossing their heads and prancing in circles. Although Jenny had met a few, most of them were strangers, and she looked at them curiously. These were the fast ones, the experienced ones, the timid and the slow ones that she would be riding against. For some reason she felt as if she were gazing down on everyone and then she realized it was because Falla was so tall.

"I knew you were long-legged, but I didn't realize what a giant you really are," she softly remarked. Just then the bugle blew, a soprano on the loud-speaker led the crowd in "The Star Spangled Banner," and the opening parade began.

From her seat on Farfalla's back, Jenny could see it all—the flag bearers on matched white horses with banners streaming overhead; rodeo officials in antique automobiles; visiting queens from towns that had elected rodeo courts. One was in white with a maroon kerchief and pink and maroon pompoms all around the saddle blanket. Another wore yellow with a black hat over her long black hair. They all had sprays of flowers behind their saddles.

Next came the rodeo clowns; the pick-up men, who would help get riders off the broncs unhurt; the contenders—both men and girls—in plain, serviceable boots and broad-brimmed hats. Jenny rode beside Pam all the way around the arena, trying to believe she was actually there.

With the parade over, the contests began, and Jenny was glad to find that the barrel race came early—the fourth event. Between her and the arena proper was a high fence with openings for the riders to enter, through one of which she had a partial view of the races. She watched cowboys on broncos, holding the reins in one hand and swinging the other high in the air. Some riders roped calves and wrestled them to the ground. A rodeo clown did tricks with a trained pig. Every few minutes she looked at her watch, shaking it once in case it had stopped. And at last the announcement boomed over the speakers.

"Next—the teen-age barrel race. We have four-teen promising young riders, ladies and gentlemen, and fourteen lively pieces of horseflesh." The girls jammed their hats more firmly onto their heads and tightened their hold on the reins.

"As soon as the barrels are in place, they'll be off. Get it right, boys!" This last, to the young men who were setting the red, white, and blue barrels, brought a burst of laughter from the crowd.

Jenny's stomach was plunging into her boots as she watched the men roll the barrels forward and position them over markers on the ground.

"And now they're ready. The first contestant. Miss Kari Redding. On Texas.*"*

As Kari, a stranger, started forward, Jenny could

see her hands trembling. *Mine are shaky too*, she thought. *Why did I get into this, anyway?* By moving closer she could see the starter with his flag, and the finish, but not the first barrel.

Kari rode into place. Leaned forward. Took off toward the first barrel and out of sight, while the crowd burst into a roar. And then, after only a few seconds, there was Kari, bent far over her horse's neck. He was leaning toward the second barrel, ears back, mane and tail flying. Missing it by a foot. Racing toward the last. Rounding it. Streaking for home.

"NINETEEN POINT TWO," came the voice over the speaker. Only a fair time, Jenny knew. *But I hope Falla will do as well*, she thought, as she tried to remember everything she had been told. *Hold my knees firm. Talk to him a lot. Give him that all-important kick.* "You're wonderful, Falla," she said, straightening a tangled hair of his mane. "Whether you win or not, I love you."

After several other riders, two of whom bettered Kari's time, Pam's name was called. Jenny could see her, skinny and small on Rocky's back, holding him firm.

"Good luck," Jenny called, waving her free hand. Although Rocky had often clocked an excellent time at the ranch, Mr. Winokur said the effect of a crowd on a nervous horse couldn't even be guessed, so anything might happen now. "Go, Rocky. Run your best," she called, her voice lost in the uproar.

Rocky, in the starting area, was tense and ready to

run, stepping high and tossing his head. When the flag dropped, he started as if he were on springs, and Pam was away. But in only a few seconds she had rounded the first barrel—the one that was out of sight —and was almost at the second. "Please don't bump it, Rocky," Jenny said under her breath. "At least, don't knock it over." He had done that several times at the ranch.

He was there—grazing the barrel—tipping it, and Jenny gasped. But the barrel righted itself, Rocky rounded another and was on his way home, head and neck stretched out, feet thundering, while Pam lay along his neck and yelled in his ear. Tail streaming, he crossed the finish line.

"Seventeen point six!" A wonderful time! As Pam jogged back to the staging area, Jenny put her crop between her teeth, looped the reins over her arm, and held up her clasped hands in a joyous wave.

After that came a blur of horses and riders, with no time equal to Pam's, and then, as loud as thunder and twice as terrifying, the voice of the speaker. *"Jenny Alexander. Riding Farfalla."*

"Here's our chance, Falla-boy!" she said, digging in her heels. "Let's show them what we can do."

Trembling, she rode into place. The starter raised, then dropped his hand. She kicked her heels hard. Leaned forward. "Go now! Go! Run!" she shouted.

As if he understood, Farfalla plunged ahead . . . And Jenny went blank. She forgot everything she had learned. Which barrel came first? She hadn't the faintest idea. Which side should she go around? She couldn't remember. Where next? And next? She shut her eyes and hung on tight.

"Go! Run! *Please*, Falla, run fast!" she implored. At least she was sure of one thing—*keep talking to your horse. Right into his ear.* "Please, Falla—*please* don't forget how!" She clung to the mane, felt the warm muscles surging beneath her, shouted anything that came into her head. By the time she opened her eyes again, Farfalla had rounded the first barrel and was streaking toward the next, while Jenny realized she had never gone so fast before in her whole life.

Then, all at once, memory flooded back. Of course. Here, just ahead of her, was the second barrel, and . . . yes . . . Falla, darling Falla, was doing it right. She'd help him with the rest.

She drew her reins to the side. Gave him his kick. Leaned as he rounded the barrel, so close her elbow brushed it. He crossed to the last, rounded it, and as he stretched out for the finish line, Jenny felt her hair flying as if it were in a high wind.

And there she was! She'd done it! She'd ridden her first race without any terrible mistakes—thanks to her horse. They were home.

The announcer's voice was blaring her name again. *"That was Jenny Alexander, folks, on Farfalla. Time . . . twenty point two. Jenny's first race, and Farfalla's first race, too. Let's give them a big hand."* Not a great time—she hadn't won—but she'd made the ride. I did it! she thought. I did it! I really did! She vaguely knew that the next rider had been called up on a little white mare.

When it was over, Pam was the first-place winner and received a blue rosette. Farfalla hadn't placed—but Jenny hadn't really expected him to. Finishing the course was triumph enough.

In a moment Pam's father appeared, handsome in a brand-new red and green plaid shirt, with his cowboy hat hung far back on his head. "Great race," he told Pam with a grin. "You rode him to win, and you did it. I'm proud of you." He patted Rocky, then turned toward Jenny, "You rode fine too, Jenny. Were you scared?"

"Scared? For a minute I went absolutely blank," she confessed. "Falla saved us." She had dismounted and was holding the reins just below Farfalla's chin, and now she rubbed her nose against his long muzzle.

"Smart horse," Mr. Winokur agreed. "Perhaps not a barrel racer, though. His size is against him."

"I know," Jenny sadly agreed. "He's the tallest one in this whole race."

"He's worth working with, though. Smart. Courageous. Don't give it up yet." The big man gave the horse a friendly slap on the rump, then walked away.

Next came Lissie and Chip, each holding a cloud of pink cotton candy and dancing with excitement. "Falla was *so neat!*" Lissie exclaimed. "He really can run fast."

"Pretty fast," Jenny agreed with a smile.

"I think he should have a ribbon," Chip insisted. "He didn't knock over even one single barrel."

"Not even one," Jenny said, bending down to their level. "And kids—you'll never guess what happened. *I forgot everything I knew! But Farfalla remembered.*" She told them all about the race, how it felt and what she thought.

"He ought to have a ribbon," Chip repeated.

"I could make him one," Lissie suggested. "Mommie has lots of ribbons in her scrap box. Would you like that?"

"Love it," Jenny told them.

"Will you put it on your wall?"

"If you make me a rosette, I'll put it up," Jenny promised. "I can't think of a trophy I'd rather have."

Chip wiped a wisp of cotton candy from his nose. "Let's go back to Mommie," he said. "We can see better there. Coming, Lissie?"

"Okay," Lissie replied, and they scampered off.

With the race over, Jenny stood beside Falla, talking with the other girls and catching glimpses of the action. "I think I'll go home," she soon told Pam. "I don't want to leave Falla by himself, and I can't see much from here."

"I know," Pam agreed. "Come back this afternoon."

"Will you be here?"

"Where else?" asked Pam with a grin. "The boys will watch Rocky for me, and we'll get seats in the stands. Eat hot dogs and other nourishing snacks! You can learn a lot."

"Great!" Jenny mounted Farfalla and started for the exit.

On the way out several cowboys commented on her ride. "Nice work." "Good race." One of them, an older man who looked like a ranch owner, took hold of a rein and brought Falla to a stop. "I like this fellow. Is he the mystery horse I've heard about?"

"Mystery?"

"The horse without a past? I heard there was one, owned by a visiting girl from California. A big brown gelding with white streaks up its legs."

"Well—maybe he's a mystery. But he belongs to my cousin now," Jenny replied, holding Falla on a short rein because he was tossing his head. She wanted to get away, and quickly, before the man asked any more questions. "I think he's pretty restless. I'd better take him home."

"Right. They get mighty excited," the man replied and touched his hat brim. "Luck to you. Don't be discouraged, just because you lost the first time."

"Oh, I won't," Jenny promised and thankfully started on.

As she jogged along the road, which was almost deserted now, she felt as if all her bones had turned to jelly. Nothing she had ever done, nothing in her while life, had made her so tired. But Falla—darling Falla—had done well.

Maybe too well, a voice deep inside her said. *That*

man had already heard about a mystery horse. If Falla starts winning, he'll be famous for sure. And then I'll surely have to think of a way around all these questions.

But he wasn't famous yet, and who would have guessed that this summer, which had started out in such a dumb-dumb way, would be so exciting! More than that—who would have guessed that sick, lackadaisical Horse would turn into beautiful Farfalla! So fast! So smart!

I love him so much, she thought. I want to keep him forever.

11

◆◆

Chips, Again

Horses that live in the wild learn to care for themselves, to find food, find water, and choose safe footing. They can all run, jump and make quick turns, although some are more adept than others.

YOU AND YOUR EQUINE FRIEND, page 39.

"The pond isn't very far. We can all ride Falla." Chip was glaring at Jenny, with his jaw thrust ominously forward. "I want to go today."

"It's too late in the year, Chip. By now tadpoles are half grown, and they're hard to catch. Besides, they'll be way out in the pond, out of reach."

"Not all of them. I only want a few. You *promised* you'd take me when the rodeo was over. And it is."

"I promised—yes—*if* your mother agreed. We

haven't asked her yet, and she's gone to work. So we'll have to wait."

It was Monday morning, two days after the rodeo. Jenny had already packed her lunch, ready to spend a long, lazy day in the mountains, alone with Falla. She smiled as she remembered her first week there, when she had ached for the roar of the ocean, for friendly red tile roofs, for bougainvillea and poinsettias and palm trees. Now she wanted only the sharp smell of sagebrush and the big, blue Wyoming sky. She guessed wherever you were happy was always the most beautiful place on earth.

But Chip wasn't giving up. "You can ask Mommie on the telephone."

"Not at the office, unless it's important."

"That's right," said Lissie, with an emphatic nod. "You know that, Chip. She's real busy."

Chip stood on one leg and scratched his ankle and with the opposite toe. "She won't care. She likes Falla."

"I know she does, and she'll let you go some day," said Jenny, trying to be patient. "But we have to ask her first." The children were looking up at her with their tilted blue eyes. "Your mother won't mind if you have a short ride. I'll take you to Pinnacle Rock and back," she offered. "That would be fun."

"Good!" exclaimed Lissie. "And afterwards we'll go play with Tim and Terry. They have a new tetherball."

Chip didn't answer.

"Would you like that, Chip?" Jenny asked.

He drew his eyebrows together in one of his most prodigious frowns. "You *promised* to find me some more tadpoles. You *promised*. The day mine—got—got eaten up."

Jenny sighed. Sturdiness of character was wonderful, of course, but—did Chip have to be *quite* so rugged? "I know I promised. And I'll do it. But not today."

"Well. I have to feed my rabbits." Chip stalked off with his hands in his pockets.

Lissie, however, scrambled up in front of Jenny and banged her heels against Falla's side. "Chip's always like that," she explained. "Mommie says the only way to handle him is just let him get over it by himself."

"I'm sure your Mommie knows what's best," Jenny agreed, as they started off.

Going slowly because the day was warm, she guided Falla to the jeep road that followed White Rock River, shallow and slow, with gray-green willows along its edge and thick stands of cattails. Blackbirds were whistling, dragonflies shimmered in the sun. At the fork of the old trail, she thought about exploring it but decided to wait for another day when she was alone.

Half a mile from town, the river and road both turned and meandered across a brushy plain, with greasewood shoulder-high and the yellow blaze of rabbit brush. The landmark, Pinnacle Rock, loomed up ahead of them, a pile of jagged gray spires. As usual, Jenny dismounted to pull back the wire gate, then rode on over the dusty ground of the range. The road was climbing now, and the river tumbled noisily along.

They dismounted at Pinnacle Rock to let Farfalla have a drink, while Lissie picked a fistful of Indian paint brush. Here, to the little girl's glee, a pair of bright eyes peered at them from the base of the rock, then vanished.

"Was it a bear?" she hopefully asked.

"More likely a rabbit. Or fox—or weasel—or badger," Jenny replied. "And now it's time to go back."

Twenty minutes later she watched both children cross the street to Tim and Terry's house, then turned Falla again toward the hills.

This time when she reached Pinnacle Rock she left the road and began to follow a narrow trail which climbed steadily around pyramid-shaped knolls and jagged outcroppings. Soon she passed a pine tree, and another, and more and more, until she was in a deep forest. It was high and dim and cool, the sunlight filtering weakly down, the air chilly and fragrant with pine. And still Jenny climbed, stopping only when she reached Mirror Lake, with its reflection of The Old Man at its farther end.

After sliding to the ground, taking off the saddle, and tying up her horse, Jenny ate her sandwich and apple, gave Falla the core, then lay down beside the

red-brown, scaly trunk of a pine tree. She looked up
—and up—to its top, which was swaying back and
forth, majestic and slow. How would it feel, she
wondered, to be a bird and perch on the very highest
branch? She imagined she was there, unafraid because
she could fly, safe in a little round nest. She closed her
eyes, listening to bird-songs high above, until at last
she reluctantly saddled Falla. "Time to start back,"
she said. "But I wish we could ride on forever."

Going down was quick. Almost before it seemed
possible, she was again within sight of Pinnacle Rock,
and there—it couldn't be! Jenny squinted and shaded
her eyes, for Lissie and Chip were partway up the
rock, perched on a narrow ledge. *Why* did they come
so far! she thought. And most especially, *why* did
they climb that rock! It's dangerous!

She nudged Farfalla with her heels and was riding
at rapid trot when Lissie spied her. "Jenny! We came
to meet you!" she called in her clear little voice.

"Here, Jenny! Here!" Chip was yelling too from a
perch just above Lissie.

"Careful!" Jenny shouted back as she gave Falla
another nudge.

Then it happened. One second Chip was standing
tall and waving with all his might; the next, he lost
his balance. He swayed—slipped—clutched at the
rough rock—and slid down its slanted face. Jenny
could see him scrabbling for a handhold, rolling, and
plunging over the edge with his arms and legs waving
in the air like a little bug.

She kicked Farfalla's sides. Up a rise they ran, down another, around a knoll. By the time she reached Chip, Lissie was there too.

"He—he fell!" Lissie's voice was a terrified squeak. "He was right there beside me. I told him that was high enough, but he kept on going. And he fell off."

"I saw him." Jenny's teeth were chattering. "Chip —Chip. Can you hear me? Answer me, Chip." She felt his wrist and yes—his pulse was beating although it was fast, like the ticking of a watch. As she released his arm he moaned, half-opened his eyes in a blank stare, then closed them again.

First aid! What had she learned in her class? Rub the arms and legs! Was that for a fall? Drowning? Fainting? *Why* didn't I pay more attention, Jenny thought. The only thing she was sure of was not to move him for fear of a broken neck. At least the angle of his head seemed right, which was one hopeful sign.

By now Lissie was crying, soft, little-girl whimpers. "Chip was so mad . . . because you wouldn't help find the tadpoles . . . that I said why not go to the rock and meet you." She looked straight at Jenny. "I really did remember the way. We didn't get lost. Only Chip —Chip—" She burst into fresh tears.

Jenny laid her jacket over him. "Lissie, crying won't help. And the ledge—that last ledge he fell from—isn't so terribly high. If you were on Falla's back, you could almost touch it. I think . . ." *Let this be true*, she thought. "I think he'll be all right. And there's something important you can do, if you're big enough."

Lissie's eyes opened wide. "I'm pretty big."

"Somebody has to get a doctor, and we mustn't leave Chip alone. The quickest way will be for me to go on Falla. That means—Lissie, can you stay here and watch him? If he wakes up, make sure he lies still until the doctor comes?"

"I can do that," Lissie stoutly replied. "I'll sing some songs."

"Good girl. Chip likes to hear you sing." Jenny squeezed her hand. "So I'm going, as fast as I can." She looked anxiously at the child—so little to be left alone with so much responsibility. But somebody must go, and somebody must stay.

She felt Chip's wrist again, and as before he moaned and half-opened his eyes. "It may seem like a long time, Lissie, but I'll hurry," she said. "Be sure not to move Chip. Just watch over him, and if anyone comes, show them where he is."

"I'll be sure." Lissie drew a deep breath and started a quavery song.

Now, thought Jenny, swinging into the saddle. What's the quickest way to town? The jeep road with its long dog-leg detour? Or the old trail, which she had never tried?

"Pam says it's used some," she told Falla, as she gathered up the reins. "It will be lots shorter. So I'm going to risk it. It's here—no—here. This is it, I'm sure."

She plunged down the narrow path, which was crooked but well-packed, just wide enough for a horse. With Falla going at a canter, she rounded a hill, threaded her way past a jagged gray ledge and down another, steeper slope. He dodged a twisted root, and splashed across a stream.

"Be careful," Jenny implored him. "Don't step into a hole." What was it Pam had told her? "Horses that live on a range can take care of themselves. They have enough sense to watch their footing." Well . . . she could only hope that Falla had been brought up like that.

The path briefly followed the base of a cliff, skirted a ravine, and topped a steep rise. Here a pair of antelope bounded off with a flash of their white rump patches.

And then, too suddenly for thought, a fence appeared half hidden by the brush. Of course—the fence that enclosed the range. Jenny knew there must be a gate, but Falla was going so fast and the fence was so close, that he didn't have time to stop. In one second of terror she realized that instead of slowing down—and crashing into it—he was increasing his speed.

"Falla!" she screamed clutching the saddle horn with one hand and mane with the other, for she could feel him tensing beneath her. He was going to jump! Could she remember what she had learned the few times she had jumped on Melody? *Get your weight forward.* She could almost hear Alec saying it. *Get up in the stirrups! Give your horse a chance!*

"Falla! I'll try!" she gasped as she braced her legs and leaned over his neck.

A thrust! Like the snap of a coiled spring. They were in the air. Rising. Tilting. And they were over! Farfalla had done it!

As they rounded the next hill, Jenny could see the first houses of Pine Valley. A few minutes later, having emerged onto the jeep road, she was at home, sliding off Falla's back, racing inside, shouting for Mrs. Wilson.

After that things moved in a whirl. Mrs. Wilson ran to the telephone. "The firemen want to pick you up at the corner so you can show them where Chip is," she said. "Hurry now. I'll call Lorelei, and I'll see to your horse, too. Grew up on a ranch." She was already dialing again.

Jenny raced back to the road, waited for the ambulance, hopped in while its engine roared, and rode to the rock, with a screaming fire truck and red firemen's car behind. *Please. Please. Let us be in time,* she said inwardly as they lurched over the bumps.

They found Chip lying as before, with Lissie on guard. "He woke up once. I sang him all my best songs. But he—he—didn't even care," she sobbed.

"You were wonderful, Lissie," Jenny soothed her. "I'm so proud of you and your mother will be, too."

While the ambulance attendants put Chip on a

stretcher and slid it into the vehicle, Jenny held Lissie tight, and they rode home in the back seat of the firemen's car.

"Do you think Chip will be all right?" asked Lissie in a very small voice.

Jenny gave her a reassuring squeeze. "I hope so, Lissie. He's a pretty strong little boy, and I couldn't see anything broken." *Let it be true*, she said to herself. *I couldn't bear it if Chip doesn't get well*.

She remembered the night soon after she came, when he put a rubber snake in her bed. The day he locked Lissie into her room. His stubbornness and tantrums. His maddening antics with Honey. But she also remembered his tenderness to his animals. Little as he was, he never forgot to feed them, or to let his rabbits out to play. She couldn't bear to give up Chip. "Brothers are pests," Lissie said, so softly Jenny could hardly hear. "But I didn't like to have him hurt."

"Neither did I," Jenny agreed. "The doctors at the hospital will know just what to do."

"Can we go see him?"

"Maybe not, at least today. They may not want him to have any company, just at first."

The little red car lurched over the rough road. "Hurry. Go faster," Jenny murmured under her breath. "Take us to Chip."

12

++

Ladders and Oxers, Verticals and Coops

In the ideal jump, the horse should leave the ground at the best spot to make a smooth arc over the fence. It is your job to help it do this.

YOU AND YOUR EQUINE FRIEND, page 188.

"Now tell me exactly how it happened," Mrs. Wilson said, dropping onto the sofa. The firemen had brought Jenny and Lissie home instead of to the hospital, and the baby-sitter had met them at the front door, her eyes red as if she'd been crying.

Jenny explained as calmly as she could.

"I told him and told him that was too far," said Lissie, drawing down her mouth as she did when she was trying to be grown-up. "But he was *bound* and *determined* to go way up there, so he'd be the first to see Jenny. And when he did see her—bang! Just like Humpty Dumpty."

"Oh! Oh, my!" Mrs. Wilson pulled a handkerchief

out of her apron pocket. "That poor little lamb. It just goes to show how it always pays to mind. You remember that, Lissie. Don't you ever forget it." She loudly blew her nose. "But we can't help Chip any by crying. And he's at the hospital, nice and safe, with his mommie right there, so he'll be all right. Now!" Clambering to her feet, she rubbed her hands on her apron. "How about some nice baked chicken? I've got it all ready."

"No." Lissie vigorously shook her head. "I want Chip to come home."

"He will, Lissie, just as soon as he's well enough," Jenny said, trying to sound confident.

"Your mommie's going to telephone, most any time now," Mrs. Wilson coaxed. "And that chicken's not going to be very good unless we eat it right off."

An hour later, while they were playing a listless game of Clue, the telephone at last rang, and as Mrs. Wilson listened, she broke into a beaming smile. "Lorelei! At the hospital!" she exclaimed. "He's better? Woke up enough to know you? Well, Heaven be praised! We'll all sleep like angels for news such as that."

"He's better? Honest?" asked Jenny.

Mrs. Wilson nodded, her plump face stretched in a smile. "A broken arm? Concussion? But not too bad a one?" She was still talking into the receiver. "But nothing worse? The saints in heaven were watching over him today, that's for sure." She listened again, then raised her voice in indignation. "Of *course* I don't mind! You just stay right there, and don't you worry about a thing. I'd already made up my mind to spend the night here, so the kiddies won't be alone."

When Jenny went to bed, she felt as if she were singing one of Lissie's songs. "Chip is all right, all right, all right. Chip's awake and all right, HE'S ALL RIGHT."

But she couldn't sleep, even though she squeezed her eyes tight shut, and counted sheep, and thought about irregular verbs and multiplication tables. She lived over and over the wild dash on Farfalla, the shock of seeing the fence, the way he'd gathered his feet together—and then the explosion of power as they were up and over! "Melody never felt like that! And he hasn't even been trained!" she told herself in the darkness.

The next day right after breakfast Jenny set out on Farfalla, but instead of staying on the jeep road, she turned into the old trail. Did she remember that jump right? Was it a regular range fence, shoulder-high, with all its wires in place? Or was it broken down, not high at all?

When she came to the fence, she slid off Falla's back, dropped the reins, and examined the ground. This was unmistakably the right place, for the trail was gouged on the far side where he had taken off, and gouged again where he had landed. And, yes, it was all there. High as it was, Falla had jumped it on a slope, with hardly any warning.

"You're *wonderful*! A *jumper*!" she exclaimed, tickling his nose in the way he liked best. "Just what I wanted." She was thinking hard as she jogged back to town.

She had just finished a long, excited letter to her parents when she heard Pam's voice outside and clattered downstairs to meet her. "Chip's fine—or soon will be," she said, walking beside Rocky down the lane toward the barn. "Lorelei telephoned again this morning." She described the accident and her wild ride to town.

"So I've been trying to teach him the wrong thing," she ended. "He isn't a barrel-racer at all. He's a jumper. I was a dope not to figure that out, long ago."

"He's built like one," Pam agreed. "But my dad said not to give up racing yet. There's another rodeo at Wyatt next week. We'll let him try again."

Jenny shook her head. "Pam—I'm going to give Falla a better chance than that. I'm going to set up some jumps right here in our field and practice with them every day. I've jumped a few times on Melody —she's a schooling horse at the Dexter—so I know *something* about it. And I'm going to find a horse show with events for jumpers in some town that's close enough for me to enter."

"*Jumping! Super!*" exclaimed Pam. "Let's see— they have that kind of show at the state fair and Salt Lake and Denver and a few other cities around. But the shows close by are . . . let me think. . . ." She frowned. "Well, there must be one somewhere."

"That's all right," Jenny firmly replied. "I'll find it—the state fair if I have to. I've got most of my summer money left to hire someone with a trailer to take me to it. Falla's going to have his chance—and so am I." Nothing, nothing in the world was going to change her mind.

Pam was grinning, with her eyes crinkled to crescents. "Great! I'll let Rocky try it too. Your yard here—well, it's none too big. But we can put jumps all around the edge. I'll get some bales of straw from our ranch and boards to build . . ."

Jenny gulped. "You're a mile and a half ahead of me!" she exclaimed. Pam and her instant plans! "But —yes—we'll do it!" Although she was trying to be calm, in her mind she could see Farfalla already, soaring over the jumps. Luckily she'd brought her riding clothes and they were still in the bottom drawer of her chest, right where she'd put them the first night she came, so that wouldn't be a problem.

However, she didn't work out in her own field after all because Pam's father had become interested in Falla. "Jumping now, is it?" he asked with a grin. "In your back lot? We can do better than that. I'll have some obstacles set up in that vacant pasture by the barn, and Randy"—he was one of the cowboys— "will coach you a bit. He jumped in his younger days, so he'll think he's in clover."

"Super!" Jenny exclaimed.

"And if I'm not mistaken," Mr. Winokur continued, "we have some English saddles gathering dust in the loft above the tack room. There's a horse show at Aplington in a couple of weeks with classes for jumpers, so we'll try our luck there. Got to work fast. Not much time."

After that, Jenny rode to the ranch almost every day for a brief workout. "Shouldn't push your horse too much. Got to keep him fresh so he'll look lively in the ring," Randy told her. Tall and thin, with a wheezy voice, he was permanently bent—shaped like a question mark, Jenny thought.

Having once ridden jumpers, he told Jenny exactly what to expect. "Simple obstacles, junior class. Some ladders—they look like just what they sound. Oxers—they come in pairs, to make the horse jump a long way forward. Coops—slanty—like a chicken coop. Verticals—straight up. You know about all those?"

Jenny nodded. "I've jumped them, but not on a big horse like Falla. And I've never been in a show."

"Good. We won't have regulation ones—too expensive. But we'll rig up something that's close enough for your horse to practice on. You know about flying lead changes?"

She nodded again. "That's when they turn the opposite direction and have to change which foot goes first. Falla can do it fine—I noticed that in the barrel race."

Randy grinned. "Better'n better. Some horses have a time with it. He's going to get along all right."

So Jenny and Falla began to train together. Over

the jumps: a rack of poles—hay bales, disguised with leaves—boards at a slant—brush. Before every obstacle she tried to let Falla go faster to lengthen his stride, or hold him back to shorten it, so he could take off from just the right spot. To squeeze his sides at the best possible moment. To thrust herself forward, up and off the saddle, at the exact fraction of a second that helped him most. And to sit back into the saddle just right. Will I *ever* learn that? she wondered, as she came down too soon—again—with a tooth-knocking bounce.

The hardest thing was the "in and out," two fences with a short space between, in which the horse was supposed to take one stride and no more. Jenny finally gave up trying to help Falla on this and merely let the reins go slack so he could plan his own jump.

"He's doing fine," Randy told her, moving the obstacles every day to give her lots of practice.

Although at first Pam put Rocky over the jumps, too, she soon gave up. "He's absolutely not built for this," she declared. "Barrel racing is more his style."

"Well—maybe so," Jenny agreed, thinking how Farfalla, right from the start, frolicked over the obstacles as if he liked the high ones best of all.

Five days passed. Chip came home, swaggering with importance, carrying his arm in a cast, and telling tall tales about hospital life.

A week was gone. Jenny's parents returned from Korea, and Jenny had a long talk with them on the telephone. Yes, she'd had a wonderful summer. No, she wasn't ready to leave Pine Valley. She didn't want to come home until the very last thing, just before school started. She had a wonderful horse. Could she bring him along?

"We'll see about that," her mother said. "A horse is a lot of trouble." At least she didn't—quite—say no, thought Jenny, as she saddled Farfalla for their next session with Randy.

And then, before it seemed possible, the second week was gone, too. It was time for the Aplington Horse Show.

Jenny was up at dawn to oil Falla's hoofs and shampoo his mane and tail. Randy had offered to braid them for her, but she'd said no, she could do it herself. After all, her book explained exactly how, so she hummed softly as she carried it to the back lot and tied Falla to one of the rings.

"After shampooing the tail, separate the hairs into bunches and shake out the water," she read aloud. Like this, she guessed, giving it a quick flip. "Put on the bandages." She had rags ready and quickly wrapped the tail, then washed the mane.

When that was clean and brushed smooth, she unwound the bandages. "Hey, there—easy," she told Falla, who was jerking his head. "I know you've stood here a long time, but be patient a little longer." She brushed the tail until every hair was smooth and separate. "And now for the braids."

These pictures didn't look quite the same as the braids she knew how to make, but she separated the hairs into several segments, like the diagram, and tried to cross them just right. "Not that," she said to herself, biting her lips. "Nor that . . . nor that, either." They refused to lie smooth.

"This is harder than it looks," she told Falla as she tried once more.

"Well!" she exclaimed after her fourth attempt. "The book says it will make a handsome rope, but this is more like a bunch of grapes. And it's all off to one side, with hairs sticking out all over. But it's the best I can do, so now I'll fix your mane."

However, this was so confusing that she soon gave up. "You'll just have to wear your mane loose," she told the horse. "It's clean and shiny, at least." She oiled his hoofs, and by the time Mr. Winokur, with Pam and Randy, came down the lane, she was dressed in her jodhpurs and jacket, its sleeves a bit too short, with hat and boots in her hand.

"You—er—braided his tail?" asked Randy, leading Falla toward the truck.

"I—I had a little trouble," she confessed.

"Hm-m," he wheezed. "Let's leave it loose. Don't have time to do it up now." Handing Jenny the rope, he quickly untied the ribbon and shook the hairs free, although they were still crimped at the top. "We'll brush it out smoother when we get there."

"I guess I'm not much of a hairdresser for a horse," Jenny said.

"Well . . . it takes a little practice."

By coaxing him with a carrot they soon had Falla

up the ramp and into the trailer and were ready for the ninety-mile ride. Lorelei and the children stood on the steps and waved.

"I hope you win a ribbon," Lissie shouted.

"We'll be watching!" added Chip. They would follow later on, in Lorelei's car.

It was a cool, bright morning, still quite early. Randy sat in back, Pam and Jenny beside Mr. Winokur in front, with Pam holding tightly to Jenny's hand. Nobody talked much. Now and then Jenny glanced at the rounded nose of Falla's trailer, which showed in the rear window, swaying from side to side.

As the truck rumbled along, Jenny turned over and over an idea that had troubled her ever since the week before, when Mr. Winokur had bought a new horse. Pam had told her all about it and about putting the bill of sale in the bank. *In the bank.* So a bill of sale must be important. But Jenny didn't have anything like that.

"Mr. Winokur, if I really owned Falla, would I have some kind of papers?" she asked. "A bill of sale?"

"Probably so," he replied. "Signed by the former owner."

"And if I don't have one—what then?"

He shifted gears on a hill. "Nothing much. You'll need a health certificate to cross a state line—they stop trucks to check—but you can get that all right from Falla's doctor. In all likelihood it will list you as owner. The rules for horses aren't as stringent as for cars, although . . . " He glanced at her and chuckled. "Folks out here don't have much use for horse thieves."

Thieves! The grinding noise of the truck seemed suddenly loud. "I wish I had a paper," Jenny said. "Then I'd be sure Farfalla's owner wouldn't find him and take him away."

"Well—nobody's after him so far. We'll cross that bridge when we come to it," Mr. Winokur replied, not chuckling now. "For today, all you have to do is steer him around the course."

"I'll try," Jenny promised. She'd do her very best to think only about Falla and helping him over the jumps.

And she'd soon be having to do more than just think about it, because they were passing a sign, a big one, with a bright red arrow. APLINGTON, it said. HORSE SHOW, ONE MILE.

Jenny was almost there.

13

Whose Horse?

*In a timed jump-off, the horse that can clear
the obstacles cleanly is almost certain to finish
in the ribbons.*

YOU AND YOUR EQUINE FRIEND, page 185.

As soon as Mr. Winokur reached the show
grounds, he and Randy unloaded Farfalla, who stood
quietly, ears pricked, interested, apparently none the
worse for his ride. Jenny, Pam and Randy dampened
his mane and tail and brushed them as smooth as they
could, although the crimped tail stuck out like a bush.

"It looked so easy, in the book," Jenny remarked,
as she carefully freed a stubborn knot.

Pam shrugged. "You never know til you try."

Even though Aplington was a small "C show," it
had drawn a well-dressed, prosperous-looking crowd,
who were strolling around or gathered in groups.
Horses were everywhere—stocky ponies, slim-legged

thoroughbreds, powerful hunters—being brushed or warmed up or admired. Their tails were braided, manes tied with ribbons, and as Jenny rode Falla at a walk, getting him used to the crowd, she realized that people were staring at his bushy hair.

"Odd! But a fine-looking animal!" exclaimed a woman who was carrying a notebook and camera. "Have you ridden him here before?"

"Oh, no," Jenny replied. "I'm just visiting for the summer."

"You brought your horse with you?"

"Well, not exactly. This is . . ." Falla circled, giving her an excuse to stop talking. "He's my cousin's horse," she finished when he was quiet again.

Another woman, who was clinging to the arm of a tall young man, stroked Falla's nose. "I like him— he has real class. Who bred him, may I ask?"

This time Jenny gave him a surreptitious nudge that set him prancing again. "I don't know," she called over her shoulder. "He belongs to my cousin."

The woman smiled and strolled on, but Jenny was troubled. *Tricks and running away and little white lies*, she thought. *I don't like it.*

Mr. Winokur had entered Falla in only two events, both for riders thirteen or younger, and when Jenny finished a circuit of the field, he carefully explained them:

The first was "Novice Over Fences," for riders who had never won a ribbon in an accredited show. It was a simple course and would be judged on a point system by how evenly and well the horse made the jumps, by the skill of the rider, and by general appearance.

The second was "Open Over Fences." All younger riders, even those who had won ribbons, could enter this one, which was slightly more difficult and required two rounds. That is, those who had a clean round without brushing any obstacles would compete in a jump-off, which would be timed. "Not many of the youngsters' events use a jump-off," he said, "but that's the way they do it here. Might give Falla a good chance, fast as he is."

Falla—my Falla—will do well, if he has a chance, thought Jenny, just as the bugle blew a fanfare, the signal to begin. Gathering up the reins, she lifted her hand to Pam and her father and rode timidly into the ring.

Twenty-two children were there with her—Jenny counted—ranging from about seven or eight years old to her own age. She particularly noticed one small boy on a sleek gray pony, who showed by his posture and the way he held his hands that he had been well taught. Most of them were beautifully turned out, with tailored jackets, polished leather boots, gloves, and sleek new hats. One girl was all in pink—suit, necktie, hat, with matching saddle blanket. Another wore pale blue with a dark blue neckerchief. By contrast, Jenny's too-short sleeves, worn hat, and dull rubber boots seemed positively scruffy.

"I wish I could have managed that braid—but

you're so wonderful it won't matter," she murmured, giving Falla an extra pat.

"Here's what you do," the judge—a young woman on a big black gelding—told them. "Take a canter first, a small circle, clockwise, right here at the start of the course, to get your horse warmed up. Then down the field, with a ladder and oxer on the first side, turn right onto the diagonal, with a coop and an in-and-out, straight to the far corner. You've a left turn there, another coop, a ladder, and then canter along the far fence, and a trot to finish up. Got it?"

Looking scared, the children nodded, and the first rider took off, while Jenny wondered how she could *possibly* remember all that.

Having drawn third start, she watched the first two with extra care. And it was simple, after all. Speed wouldn't count. She just had to canter in a small circle, then ride straight down one side, cross on a diagonal, and ride along the other side, taking all the jumps as they came. She could do that. She and Farfalla.

Now the second rider was finished, which meant it was Jenny's turn. Although at first her breath kept getting caught in her throat, by the time she finished the canter, she was calm again. It was actually fun! Falla was going beautifully, with springy steps, head up, ears pricked, as if he knew he was doing something special. Now for the jumps!

Down the field to the first obstacle, a ladder, its crossbars not quite the same as the home-built one on the ranch, but Falla made a perfect take-off. She rose in the stirrups. They were over! It was easy, Jenny thought, not high at all, and she'd come back to the saddle just right.

Next, the oxer, its two parts not nearly as far apart as the ones Randy had set.

The turn, with Falla on the correct lead! Darling Falla!

The coop, almost like the one Randy had made with a real chicken coop. Falla hesitated only once, at a simulated brick wall, and even there he was up and over with nothing worse than a snort, a toss of his head, and a momentary slowing down.

Now the in-and-out. *Only one stride*, Jenny pleaded, but silently—no yelling in his ear for this show. He was over the first . . . a single stride . . . and over the second. Perfect!

Around the corner, changing leads with only the slightest lurch.

Over the next coop . . . the final ladder . . . and Jenny's trial was over. It had gone well, she thought, but then, most of the young riders had done it well.

As she expected, she was not called up to receive a ribbon. So many had made a perfect run that all the places had been decided by polished technique and equipment.

"It's my fault, not yours," she told Farfalla as she patted his withers. "You didn't joggle a single one. But my hands and all aren't right yet, and you aren't braided, and my clothes are half worn out. We'll practice together with Alec this fall until we're *really* good, and we'll get better equipment, too. At least . . . I hope we will."

For the next hour she unsaddled Falla to let him rest a bit, then put on the saddle again and rode just enough to warm him up. When her second event was called, she saw that only a dozen had entered, most of them about her age. This course would be much like the first, except the obstacles were higher. Just what I want, Jenny thought. High jumps will show how wonderful Falla really is.

The trials began. The first rider rode a clean round. So did the second. The third, a tall boy on a palomino mare, knocked off a slat, which set off a chain of mistakes. Two girls brushed a barrier, one gray pony with a white tail refused a wall and had to be put at it again. But Falla, familiar now with all the obstacles, made a clean round, and Jenny was called up to ride in the jump-off.

For this, the height of the obstacles was increased, and they were moved into a different pattern, with a new course to learn. "Take a reverse at the end," the judge told them. "Come back over the same jumps in the opposite direction. You'll be timed. The fastest one to ride a clean round will win."

Patting Falla's withers, Jenny waited eagerly for her turn.

The first rider knocked off a rail. The second made a clean run, and the third. The fourth had a refusal. And at last it was Jenny's turn.

Sitting her straightest, she nudged Falla with her knees. They were off. Around the circle in a canter, then down the side, keeping to the edge, aiming at the center of the jumps.

Over a coop . . . a vertical . . . into the in-and-out without losing a second.

Over the oxer . . . the ladder, with Falla eager and unafraid.

Another oxer.

A quick reverse—the barrel-racing helped here— and they were on the way back. Falla stretched out and ran, doing the course perfectly, without brushing a single fence.

When it was over, speed had counted, not technique or equipment—and Jenny had won!

As she rode Falla away from the judge's box, proudly carrying a silver cup and shirred blue rosette, Chip and Lissie were waiting with Lorelei close by. "Neat-oh!" Chip said. His arm was still in the cast, which by now was covered with felt pen drawings.

"You've got a *ribbon*! And a *cup*! Let me *see*!" Lissie exclaimed, so Jenny handed them down.

While they were talking, a reporter approached. "How old is your horse? Did you train him yourself?" he asked, scribbling on a yellow note pad. Jenny guarded her replies, careful not to tell too much.

As the reporter turned away, he noticed Chip's cast. "Hey, young fellow. What happened to you?"

"I fell off Pinnacle Rock. So Falla took Jenny for the doctor. That's how we found out he could jump," Chip replied in his most piercing voice.

"Found out! Didn't you know?" The reporter said, bending toward him with a grin.

"Nope," Chip shrilled. "The Browns didn't tell us. They . . ."

"Chip!" Jenny interrupted. If he keeps on, they'll put it in the paper, and Falla's owners will find him, she thought. They'll take him back, now that he's won a prize. "Chip," she said again. "I think your mother . . ."

She stopped. Was this what she really wanted? To dodge people forever? Make Falla prance and circle away every time a question came close to the truth? Invent answers that were half a lie? She imagined years of worry, of heart-in-the-mouth fears every time a stranger knocked on the door or an unexpected letter came in the mail. How could she enjoy Falla with a life like that! In a sudden blinding flash she knew what she must do, and it made as complete a reverse in her mind as Falla had made in the jumpoff. *I've got to find out about him, or he'll never quite belong to me,* she thought. *Let the kids tell the whole story, and I'll help them out.*

"It's all right, Chip," she told him with a smile that felt like cardboard. "I think the man would like to hear all about it."

"Oh!" Chip raised his voice another notch. "Well

—the Browns left him in our barn when they moved out. And they told me and Lissie to look there. And we did. And there was Falla."

Lissie was talking, too. "He was standing right there, only he didn't have a name then, and besides he was sick," she said.

"So—a surprise?" the reporter asked, with an inquiring look at Jenny. "Sick? Abandoned? And you didn't know he could jump?"

"That's right." Jenny couldn't find words to say more.

"Well—quite a tale." The reporter turned around. "Hey, Sally! Here's that feature you've been hunting for. It's a wow!"

At this a brisk young woman carrying a TV camera joined them, and Jenny soon found herself besieged. Holding her back as straight as a ruler, forcing her lips to keep that cardboard smile, she answered them all and posed for pictures with Farfalla. It felt good. Clean, somehow. Like getting a lungful of fresh air after a long day in a stuffy room.

But when they were on their way home in the truck, Pam was indignant. "Being on TV is exciting. I know that," she said. "But Jenny! You spilled the whole story! We were going to keep it quiet!"

"I know," Jenny calmly replied.

"But . . . but . . ." Pam was spluttering. "Don't you see? If you want to lose Falla, that's the way."

"I didn't forget."

"Then why, for Pete's sake?"

"I just want to have it all straight." Jenny couldn't explain it any better than that.

The next evening, Sunday, when the early news came on, the family settled down in front of the set, the children excited, and Jenny full of dread. After an interminably long segment of news, the expected announcement began. "Now, for a change of pace, the biggest little horse show in Wyoming and its mystery horse. Let's go to Ted DePresne in Aplington."

And there it was: The small town. The gathering of fans. A little girl on a black Shetland. The boy who won. Some adult riders. A group of jumpers.

And Jenny! She was sitting splendidly erect on Farfalla's back, holding the blue rosette and silver cup.

"Neat-oh!" exclaimed Chip, banging his cast on the arm of his chair. "Lookit Jenny!"

Next the camera turned toward Chip, showing off his cast, and Lissie, rushing up to pat Farfalla's nose. The children told how they had found him standing in the barn, what Mr. Brown had said, and how Falla had jumped the fence after Chip was hurt. There was another picture of Jenny, smiling, answering questions, and a close-up of the horse with his ears pricked.

"So there you have it," the announcer finished, "the story of the mystery horse who won a race, and his plucky young rider. And now, after a brief pause . . ."

Jenny didn't listen to more. It couldn't be called back. It was done and on the air for anybody, anywhere to see. The whole world, she guessed, at least this part of it, might soon find out all about Farfalla. Who could say what might happen next?

14

✦✦✦✦✦✦✦✦✦✦✦✦✦✦✦✦✦✦✦✦✦✦✦✦✦✦✦✦✦✦✦✦✦✦✦✦✦✦✦

What Jenny Did

Because your horse's eyes are near the sides of his head, things look different to him than they do to you. He has poor perception of depth, but his night vision is better than yours.
YOU AND YOUR EQUINE FRIEND, page 193.

The following Saturday morning Jenny was nearly dressed when Chip and Lissie came banging up the stairs. "Jenny—telephone!" Chip was squeaking with excitement. "And we're having *pancakes*."

"Mommie says it's *long distance!*" Lissie added, as they burst through the door. "Hurry up! It's *important!*"

"Okay—okay," Jenny replied with a smile. "I'm on my way."

She dashed down the stairs, wondering what it could be. Mom? Dad? Probably, since she'd written

178 : Somebody's Horse

a long letter last week, imploring them to let her bring Falla to California. She'd reminded them that the Dexter charged much less than full board if the owner did most of the work and said she'd be *glad* to do that. They were home from Korea and should have the letter by now. Could they be calling to say it would be okay? That she should start making plans?

In the kitchen she found Lorelei holding a pancake turner in one hand and the telephone extension in the other, while dollar-size cakes sizzled on the stove. "Here comes Jenny," she said. "I'll let you talk with her direct." Handing over the receiver, she filled the children's plates and spooned more batter onto the griddle.

"Jenny? I'm McEwen. Rob McEwen, calling from Rawlins." As soon as Jenny heard the deep voice on the line, her hands turned cold. "I'd like to see you tomorrow morning, if you've got time."

"Well . . . I think so," she replied, sinking into her chair. "What—what's it about?"

The man cleared his throat. "Your horse. I saw him on television last week, from my place in Colorado, and I recognized him right off. So I decided to pay a little visit to my brother here in Rock Springs —not too far from Pine Valley—and I brought along some pictures."

"Pictures?"

"Of the animal—Farfalla, you call him? Good name. Good horse, too. I ought to know. I raised him."

"You're—sure?" Jenny could almost hear her whole world tumbling down around her ears.

"Sure as I am of my own name. I raise jumpers, and he was one of my colts. Nice little fellow. Good disposition. He was a yearling, and we'd arranged to sell him to a woman in the East—just six years ago, it was. But when I went to bring him in from the field, he was gone. Never did find out what happened, though we could guess."

"Maybe wolves got him," Jenny desperately suggested, while Chip and Lissie stopped eating, with their forks halfway to their mouths.

"Wolves?" Chip silently formed the word.

The man on the telephone laughed. "Wolves? Not a chance. He was in a field along with the other colts, and they were all right. If wolves got him, we'd have found what was left of his carcass, but that wasn't anywhere around, either. So—if it's agreeable to you, I'd like to bring my pictures over to your place tomorrow. Okay?"

"Well . . . yes. Of course." Jenny was trembling so hard she could scarcely hold the receiver. "But Mr. McEwen, why do you think Farfalla is yours?" Stupid question, she thought, even as she asked it.

The man laughed again. "Easy. By the streaks up his legs, just a bit higher on the left. And by the star, the one you think looks like a butterfly. You'll see plain enough in the pictures."

"All—all right, then. Tomorrow," Jenny agreed, and the call was over.

"He thinks Farfalla is his," she told Lorelei as she stood up to replace the telephone. "He wants to come tomorrow and show me some pictures."

"I know. He told me that, too."

"Is he going to take Farfalla away?" Lissie asked.

"Jenny, will you let him?"

"Not if I can help it," Jenny replied, returning to her chair. *Why* had she been so noble about that silly TV program? Did she think she was Mahatma Gandhi? "I'll think of something. Buy him, if I can get enough money." Fat chance, she bitterly thought.

"You can have what's in my bank," Lissie said, her blue eyes round. "I don't want him to take Falla."

"Me, either," echoed Chip. When Honey squawked "Ah-oh," he got up without being told, stalked to the cage, and threw the shawl over it. "Shut up!" he hissed.

Jenny hardly heard. "I don't think it's even the same horse," she said, wishing she could believe her own words. "How could he be so sure?"

"Jenny," Lorelei began, "did Mr. McEwen say when his animal was stolen?"

"Six years ago." Jenny took a sip of milk. "But that's a long time. I'll bet when he saw Farfalla on the tube he liked his looks, so he's made up a story."

Lorelei sighed. "You may be right, Jenny, and I hope you are. But if so, he made a lucky guess about Farfalla's age. Didn't Dr. Mike say he's seven?"

"Well—yes."

"And did you mention his age on the air? I can't seem to recall it."

"No. But lots of people know how old Falla is. It would be easy to find out," Jenny doggedly replied. "That's no proof."

Lorelei lifted the edge of a browning pancake. "Jenny, don't think I'm on his side. But he says his pictures show the stripes and the butterfly. How distinctive are marks like those?"

"A few horses have stripes, but I've never seen another butterfly. Maybe he's right," Jenny reluctantly admitted. "Just the same, Falla is *my horse* and he can't have him." Although Lorelei handed her a plate of steaming pancakes, she only gazed at them, without picking up her fork. *Dummy!* she was calling herself. *Dumb! Dumb! Dumb!* to get into this mess.

Chip tried to divert her with a story. "Do you know what the flea said when the elephant sat on it?"

Jenny stared. "I'm sorry, Chip. I wasn't listening."

When he repeated the question, she said she couldn't possibly guess. "You must have packed your trunk!" he shouted, doubling up with giggles.

"I know one, too," Lissie countered. "It's about a man that had a wooden pump. It wooden pump!" She waited a moment, then asked, "Get it, Jenny? It *wooden pump!* That means it—"

"I get it," Jenny said, with an attempt to smile. "That's a pretty good joke, Lissie." Jokes! she thought. While her life was caving in!

"How about my joke?" Chip demanded. "Isn't it a good one, too?"

"It is—but out you go, both of you!" Lorelei ordered. "You're stuffed, and Jenny needs some time to herself." She gave them each a quick hug, and then, as they banged the door, she dropped into a chair opposite Jenny's. "We'll try not to be too worried until we can see this Mr. McEwen," she said.

"Do you think there's any chance that he won't want Farfalla?" Jenny asked, as calmly as she could.

"I honestly don't know. Horses, ranches, all that —they're beyond me. But, Jenny, we'll have to face it—Falla may be too valuable for him to give up."

"Do you think he's worth a lot, really a *lot* of money?"

"Possibly. Pam's father could tell you more about that than I can. But Jenny—let's not borrow trouble. We don't know that he's going to take your horse. It may all be a mistake, or he may be merely curious to find out what happened.

"You don't really think that. Do you?" How could Lorelei be so calm, as if she were talking about a problem in geometry? "*Do you?*" Jenny repeated.

"Well—no. But I think you'll have to show him Farfalla and see what can be done."

"It's easy for you to say that—and sit there all nice and peaceful—and not really care!" Jenny burst out, knowing how unreasonable she was, yet unable to stop. "It isn't *your horse!*"

"Jenny—that isn't quite fair." Lorelei sounded almost angry. "I do care. I care a lot. But I know what's possible and what isn't, and I know we have to see Mr. McEwen and works things out with him."

"He'll try to take Falla. I know he will." Jenny felt as if she were strangling on her own words. "But he can't! I'll—I'll hide him!" She jumped up and flung down her napkin. "I'll move him so far away he won't ever find him! He *can't have my horse!*" Stifling a sob, she ran through the door and pounded up the stairs.

Twenty minutes later she quietly returned, her mind made up. She wasn't going to beg and whine, that was sure, but neither was she giving up. She didn't know how she'd do it, but some way—somehow—she was going to figure out a plan.

For right now, she'd have a good long ride on Farfalla, all by herself, so she could think. She could hear the rattle of Lorelei's typewriter—working on the book, of course. No use to bother her. Jenny slapped together a couple of thick cheese sandwiches, put them into a plastic bag, and ran outside.

It was a warm day, and the sky was heavy with gray-white clouds, pile upon pile, rolling through the dazzling blue. Would it rain in the mountains? she wondered, and deciding it might, she pulled her sweater and hooded rain jacket off their hook and fastened them behind the saddle. She put the sandwiches into the saddle bag and tied on Falla's halter and rope, in case she wanted to let him graze.

Going slowly because it was so warm, she followed

the jeep road toward Pinnacle Rock, but today she wasn't interested in the river, or birds, or flowers. It wasn't fair, she brooded, as she jogged along in the dust, staring at her own hands. Falla was really hers. She'd saved him twice—first from the packing plant, and then when he was sick. And now a stranger who hadn't see him for six years was coming. He'd claim him. She knew he would. Anybody would want a horse like Falla, and Pam's father, that day in the truck, had talked about bills of sale, as if the horse didn't really belong to her.

At Pinnacle Rock, Jenny turned off the road and headed up the narrow trail she had followed once before. She'd like to see some really wild country today—the wilder the better—and if she met a cougar, or a bear, that would be fine, too. She'd go away up to Mirror Lake—and beyond. Pam had told her about a high waterfall above the lake, in rough country. Well, that was fine with Jenny. Just what she needed. Up there, where it was high and clear and cool, with a roaring torrent to sit beside, she might be able to think. She remembered the way: along this narrow path, then left at the fork, toward The Old Man.

At first Jenny's trail wound between hummocky hills, dry and brown so late in the summer, with a scattering of head-high brush and rough, gray rocks. In the hollows she felt closed in and breathless, but whenever she went over a rise, a stiff breeze cooled her burning face. From the highest knolls she could look back at the valley, which was in brilliant sun, splotched with lavender cloud shadows that drifted slowly past. For a long time, whenever she looked back, she could see Pinnacle Rock standing high and craggy above all the rest, but as the path worked its way around the shoulder of a mountain, the rock was lost. Without it Jenny felt forsaken, as if she'd been set adrift.

The trail was climbing steeply now, its vegetation slowly changing from juniper and greasewood to pines and firs—solitary small ones at first, then groups, until Jenny was riding on a springy path through a forest. Soft light filtered down; it was higher here, shady and cool at last, but even in this clear air she found it hard to think. She had to keep Falla somehow. What was she going to do?

She rode blindly along. Coming to a little brown stream, she let Farfalla splash across and take a drink . . . and she was hardly aware that he had stopped. When he shook his head and tugged at the bit, she relaxed the reins and he was off on a swift canter. Although she swung with his rocking motion, she paid him almost no attention, letting him go as he wished.

And suddenly—there was Mirror Lake, a shining oval bowl with evergreens all around its edge and a red bluff at one side. But today the water was silvery gray instead of blue, with the Old Man half hidden by clouds. Troubled as Jenny was, she caught her breath at the beauty of the place.

"We're here!" she told Falla. "Time for lunch!"
Slipping off his saddle and bridle, she tied him to a
tree beside a patch of grass—how lucky she'd brought
the halter and rope—then sat down with her back
against a rock and nibbled one of her sandwiches.
Even now, after the long ride and no breakfast, she
wasn't hungry. Where could she hide Farfalla, she
wondered, as she gazed at the lake. And, if she did
manage to spirit him away, how could she feed him
and shoe him and pay for his doctor bills? What was
she going to do?

If was as if a voice from somewhere inside herself
answered: *Do? You're going to go back, that's what,
and see this Mr. McEwen and find out what he wants.*

But he'll claim Falla.

*That's right. But at least you won't be scared of
the doorbell for the rest of your life.*

Falla's mine. I saved him.

*You know he isn't yours. Not really. But if you see
this man, then you have a chance—not much of a
chance, but the only possible one—to be the real
owner.*

I can't bear to lose Falla.

It works better to get things straight.

Well, Jenny decided, she'd have to think about it
some more. Meanwhile, for right now, she was up
here in the mountains, she'd never seen that waterfall,
and for once she had plenty of time.

"We'll find it," she told Farfalla, who was quietly
nibbling a clump of grass. She glanced at a steep slope

that began at the lake's edge and rose through the trees, up and up until it was out of sight. "Pam said it was above the lake, on the highest side, so it must be that way. She said I could hear it, pretty soon." Resaddling the horse, she swung to his back, and they started out.

Although there was no trail, the trees were widely spaced like a park, with very little undergrowth, and Jenny guided Farfalla back and forth in a series of switchbacks between the towering trunks. She rode up a slope, down, then upward again, working her way constantly higher. Beautiful as the mountain was, she found it sad too. Would this be the last time they could come here together, she and Farfalla?

"I think I hear water now," she told him. "It's off toward that side." She rode to the right, only to be blocked by a canyon, and when she tried to follow it, thick brush grew all along its edge. "The waterfall must be down below," she said. "Maybe we can find its upper end instead." Turning aside, she worked her way higher still.

By now Jenny had left the lake far behind and had climbed so high that the air was cold. She reached back for her sweater and wriggled into it.

"Here's a cliff, sort of. Let's see if we can look out over the valley," she said, guiding Farfalla to the edge. On a clear day she would have had an open view, but now she could see only banks of cloud filling all the low places, as if they were a chain of gray lakes, while streamers of fog swirled in and out among the hills. The sun had disappeared, and a heavy sky lay overhead like the drab ceiling of an enormous room. While she sat there, she felt a cold drop on her forehead, then another. A thin rain had begun to fall.

"It's all gray—just like I feel," she said as she turned Farfalla around. "We'd better start back. If we go down to the lake, we can find the trail there."

But nothing looked familiar—or everything was the same. She passed rounded knolls, veiled by rain; towering trees, their tops lost in fog; dripping rocks.

"We came this way—or was it that?" she asked Farfalla. "Somehow this doesn't look right. But then, maybe I just don't remember. We'll be okay. All we have to do is find the lake and follow along its shoreline until we come to the trail."

Falla tossed his head.

As they plodded on, Jenny lost her sense of direction. She couldn't see far, and the hills tricked her. What seemed to be a downward course would abruptly reach bottom and start up again, higher than before. Because of the slopes and outcropping rocks, she couldn't go in a straight line, but turned blindly back and forth.

Big as it was, the lake didn't appear, although she had searched for a long time. "I have to find it— that's the only way to the trail," Jenny said, as she put the plastic jacket on over her sweater and pulled up the hood. "But with no sun—and no view of the valley—and no snowcaps in sight—I can't tell which way—" Her voice faded.

By the end of another hour she was sure that instead of working her way down, she was rising again. Was she headed higher into the mountains? How could she know, when hills and cliffs and ravines were everywhere, all mixed up and all alike?

Just as she pulled Falla to a halt, rain began to fall harder, with a whine of wind and heavy drops that plopped onto her hood. "Falla—you'll be so cold!" she exclaimed. "I didn't bring your blanket. And I'm almost sure this is taking us up, not down. We'd better try the other way."

Pulling her chin into her collar, she turned her horse around. It was raining; it would soon be dark. She was lost.

15

✦✦

In the Mountains

*The intelligence of some horses is astounding.
Sometimes you may feel that your horse
knows more than you do.*

YOU AND YOUR EQUINE FRIEND, page 198.

"Falla! Hurry! Faster! Faster!" Jenny
crouched over his neck. She'd been trying to find her
way out—forever, it seemed—but she couldn't tell
north from south, up from down, because all the
downhill slopes seemed to end with a rise. If she
could find a stream, she could follow it to the valley,
but the only water was the cold rain that rattled on
her plastic rain jacket. She was lost . . . lost in the
mountains. It was dusk. And unless she found her
way out soon, she'd have to stay there all night.

"*Run!*" Forgetting everything she knew about
riding, Jenny clutched the saddle horn and kicked
with both heels, sending Falla into a reckless canter.

Around a rock. Up a rise. Down a slope. And then he was in the air, leaping over a fallen tree that was half hidden on the forest floor. "Run! Falla—run!" She huddled in the saddle as the horse continued his frantic dash through the rain. Branches snapped under his feet; something tore at her clothes; she screamed in terror.

But such a wild flight couldn't last, and before long, Farfalla's sides were heaving. "I'm *sorry*," Jenny murmured then, relaxing the reins. "What a dumb thing to do." Her voice dropped to a whisper because, now that they had slowed down, the monotonous drumming of rain and moaning of wind in the trees gave her the feeling that something was there, all around in the gray woods. "I've got to *think!*" Farfalla plodded sedately on, feet squelching on the sodden forest floor. His coat was shiny-wet, his mane clumped together in strands, and even in her sweater and jacket, Jenny was shivering with cold.

However, she was over her panic. "There must be some way to get out of here," she said. "It's summer . . . we won't freeze. We can go without eating, at least for today. And water . . . well, there's plenty of that coming right down on top of us. If we can just keep calm, Lorelei will soon have people out searching. Only the rain will wash out our trail. And Falla —we have to stay here all night." Her voice quavered. "It's soon going to get dark. We haven't a flashlight, or even a match."

Falla tossed his head and nickered.

As they plopped along, Jenny went over every plan she had ever heard for finding your way. *Steer by the sun*—but she couldn't do that, when it was behind a gray veil of clouds. *Steer by the stars*—but they'd be under clouds tonight too, even if she knew which ones were which. *Follow water downhill*—but she hadn't seen a stream for ages. *Keep the snow-caps behind you*—but how could she do that when she couldn't see where they were?

"We'll keep going and hope we blunder onto a trail," she decided.

Silver, Jenny always used to think of the rain, but now it was only gray—a cold, wet curtain, drumming on all sides, shutting her off from the world. It was like being in a dream: up a rise, down a slope, turn right, turn left—with never any change. Just the mantle of rain and the cold and the steady pattering sound.

"I don't think we're getting anywhere!" she told Farfalla. "We may be going around in circles or going the opposite direction from home. But keeping on is our only chance." Farfalla trotted boldly ahead.

It was raining harder now, thudding on the forest floor, and the wind was stronger, making the fir trees sway. Great drops of water plopped on Jenny's jacket; some had leaked into the front of her hood; her hair was wet. Darkness was pressing in. She must find a place to spend the night—shelter for herself, grass for Falla, and water for both of them. Maybe she could take off her jacket and collect some of the rain in that.

Just as she was about to try it, Falla pricked his ears, tugged on the bit, and turned strongly toward the left. "Do you *hear* something?" she asked, surprised, but gave him his head, and in a few minutes he stopped beside a little spring. Even though no stream ran from it to guide her downhill, it gave each of them a long refreshing drink.

"Now we'll both feel better," Jenny said.

When the horse, satisfied at last, lifted his dripping muzzle, she remounted and once more urged him ahead. "Look for an overhanging rock," she said. "We can find a little shelter there." She tried not to think how dark it would be, and how many animals lived in the woods.

When they came to the foot of a bluff, she guided Falla close, and before long, tucked into a crevice between two columns of stone, she spotted the black mouth of a cave, with a smooth patch of ground in front. "Let's try that. I'll tie you up," she told him. "Thank goodness I brought your halter and rope." Sliding to the ground, she flexed her tired legs. "Here's even some grass. Not much, but it will help. And I've got a soggy sandwich left." After tying Farfalla to a small tree, she took off the saddle, carried it to the cave mouth, and cautiously peered in. "Hello!" she called, in case an animal lived there.

Seen in the dusk, it seemed to go back and back

into blackness, an echoing dark hole with a dank, rocky, mossy smell. The instant Jenny took a timid step inside, a flight of bats swooped down from the ceiling, squeaking as they came. *I can't sleep here. I can't!* She flung herself back outside.

But the bats flew away, the rain was cold, and she was so tired that she ventured just under the opening where it was dry, but as close as possible to Farfalla. Finding a smooth spot on the floor, she dropped the saddle, sat down beside it, leaned against the wall with her knees bent, and spread the jacket over herself like a tent, shoulder to feet. Cold and wet, she huddled there in a miserable, shivering ball. After a while she found that frightened as she was, she was hungry, so she ate the rest of her lunch.

"I got settled just in time," she told herself, for by now everything was shrouded in utter blackness without a glimmer of light. Jenny hadn't known anything could be so dark. It was like ink, like black velvet, like a closet, with only the steady beat of rain, and an occasional rustle as Falla moved around. Something scurried across the cave floor, almost at her feet, and Jenny cried out. It scurried again, and was gone.

Suddenly Jenny jumped up, for she heard a terrible snarl that rose and rose to a scream, then ebbed slowly away, while Falla snorted in fear. A cougar! Jenny had heard them before, but never so close. And never before in an open cave, with nothing to keep her company except a horse tied up just outside.

"Falla?" she called, inching her way into open air. He was quiet now except for a soft whicker, then everything was still again, except the rain. He was safe, at least so far, and she was, too.

Creeping back to her level spot, Jenny tried to lie down with the saddle for a pillow, but stretching out made her so cold that she again curled up under her jacket. Miserable as she was, she finally dozed, to be awakened by a rapid *whoo-whoo-whoo-whoo* that passed the cave mouth and faded out. An owl, she thought, as she squirmed to a different position.

The long night wore slowly along, always with the sound of pounding rain. Jenny went to the cave mouth several times to call her horse and hear his reassuring snuffle. She was standing there when another cry came across the night, a steady, sharp yapping that grew into a chorus of treble shrieks and sank away. Coyotes, of course. This time Farfalla replied with a loud neigh, and she could hear his hoofs against the ground.

"Falla!" she cried. "Falla! Don't leave me!" Had he broken loose? Fearfully, in the blackness and rain she ran toward him, expecting the sound of hoofbeats in the distance, but he was still securely tied.

"Falla—my darling Falla. We're having an awful time," she murmured, patting his withers, his neck, his back, while he laid his head against her and rubbed her with his nose. Wet as he was, he felt warm to her touch.

Back in the cave, Jenny curled up again with the plastic for a cover. She was sure every thread she had on was soaked. Would this night never end? She wept. Dozed. Heard the cougar again. The coyotes. Awoke and cried and dozed some more. But at last, after another restless nap, she opened her eyes and was astonished to see a faint gray mottling of the rocky cave walls. Morning was here! Flinging off the jacket, she jumped up, stretched, and stood at the mouth of the cave, watching the forest gradually emerge in the gray light. It was still raining. But Falla, placidly having an early-morning snack of grass, was safe.

As soon as it was light enough, she saddled him, and started out. "We'll do better today, I'm sure we will," she told him. "First, let's look for a stream. That will show us the way to the valley."

Around gullies, around hills, up and over knolls she rode in the rain, losing all track of time. Twice she found a creek and started to follow it down, only to have it plunge over a waterfall and lose itself far below. She stopped several times for Falla to eat a patch of grass, but her sandwiches were gone, and she felt empty clear to her toes. Although she kept her eyes open for berries, she saw none and didn't know what else might be safe to eat. *Lorelei must have people looking for me*, she told herself. *Surely somebody will come. I'll be home tonight.*

Instead, after what seemed like an eternity, even the gray half-light began to fade, and she found refuge in another cave. "I'm so hungry—and so tired," she

told her horse. "I can't keep on like this much longer."
Curled up under the plastic, she had a broken sleep
full of dreams, awaking to find that the rain had
slackened off and the gray light of morning had
come.

"It's brighter, a little," she told Falla as she again
put on his saddle. It was heavy, so heavy. Surely it
had never been so heavy before or so hard to cinch.
"Maybe we'll find our way today," she said as she
wearily started out.

Some time later—she couldn't tell how long—as
she was trying to work her way down a steep slope,
Falla jerked at the bit and shook his head.

"Falla!" Jenny exclaimed. "What's *wrong* with
you? You act as if you don't want me to ride you
any more." She was instantly overcome with pity.
"Maybe you don't. I've been on you most of two
days, and here I am again. Maybe your poor back is
tired." Sliding off, she walked along beside him, holding the reins just under his chin. But he still tossed
his head and tried to pull her aside.

"Falla!" Jenny gave the reins a sharp jerk. "Have
you forgotten everything you ever knew! Or—!" An
idea dawned. "Maybe you know which way to go!
Maybe this seems like going *down*, but it's really *up*!
I'm going to let you choose for a while. You can't do
any worse than I have!" Clambering back into the
saddle, she sat relaxed with loose reins.

At first nothing seemed much different. Falla
trudged up the rise then on and on through the silver

tunnel of mist. Up a knoll. Down a slope, with the forest rustling all around. But—weren't the trees more sparse? Wasn't that a juniper? Yes—Jenny was sure of it. They weren't out of the forest yet, but the trees were smaller and farther apart. The mist was brightening, too, and after a while it stopped altogether. Everything was quiet except Farfalla's footsteps and the occasional plop of dripping water.

Suddenly Farfalla whinnied and broke into a canter, taking her to the edge of a bluff from which Jenny could look out over the valley. It lay below her under heavy gray clouds, and even as she sat there on Falla's back, watching with delight, the sky seemed to rise, as if someone were lifting up a mighty umbrella, or the roof of an enormous gray tent. As the clouds lifted, their edges glowed, and then . . . the sun broke through, with shafts of light like the shining spokes of a wheel.

"Now we can find our way down—I think," Jenny said. "But Falla . . . that land . . . it's so . . . so lonesome." She could see no house, no road, no sign of a human hand. Falla, however, turned his head, as if he wanted to go.

Being able to see the rocks and brush made it easier to travel. Once a deer trotted past with its head up. Again, a fox loped along, with only a quick glance for her.

And here was a trail. "It's got to go somewhere," Jenny told her horse. "We'll follow it."

Riding swiftly in the sunshine, she soon came to a

fence, which led her across rough ground with a heavy growth of brush. *Wonderful sagebrush! Wonderful mesquite!* Jenny thought. *They mean I'm out of the mountains. And super-wonderful fence! People built it! Surely it will take me to somebody!* She had ridden beside it for only a short distance, when she rounded an extra-large rock, saw an empty jeep, and a moment later came upon two men who were replacing a post.

"Hello over there! Hello!" she shouted, giving Falla a kick that sent him into a canter. "Please—what's the quickest way to Pine Valley?"

"Pine Valley?" The older man took off his hat and wiped his hand across his forehead. "That way—but it's thirty mile. You lost?"

"Yes. It was awful. And I've got to tell Lorelei I'm all right."

"Say . . ." The other man was squinting his eyes at her. "I think I saw your picture in the newscast last night. You that girl that ran off?"

"No . . . I mean yes. I guess I'm the girl," Jenny admitted. "But I didn't run away. I got lost."

"Well, I reckon we'll see you home safe and sound," said the first man. "My name's Hank—and this fellow here, the handsome one, is Bill." Bill, who had a bushy, curly red beard and a large red nose, grinned and bobbed his head. "Come along. Our jeep's over there just a piece. We'll get a truck and give you a lift."

"I can ride," Jenny protested.

"Your horse looks beat," the man briskly said. "So do you. I wouldn't want to see you start out in such shape, not even if you knew the way, which you don't."

"Well—all right." Jenny slid off Farfalla's back and handed over the reins. It would be wonderful not to worry any more or figure out which way to turn or try to find a place to sleep. "I think you're right. We do need some help."

Stumbling, she followed Hank to the jeep.

16

✦✦✦✦✦✦✦✦✦✦✦✦✦✦✦✦✦✦✦✦✦✦✦✦✦✦✦✦✦✦✦✦✦✦✦✦

Farfalla's Story

The ancient Greeks trained their horses through kindness, good food and care, and those principles still apply. The well-treated horse is almost always docile and friendly.

YOU AND YOUR EQUINE FRIEND, page 15.

Afterward, Jenny had only a hazy memory of the ride in the jeep, of stopping at a ranch and having a bowl of soup while Hank and Bill loaded Farfalla into a horse trailer. She dozed most of the way home, faintly aware that she was riding in a truck that was wonderfully dry and warm.

However, when they reached Lorelei's drive, she came wide awake because Hank began a wild honking, and by the time he stopped beside the back door, people were rushing toward them. The instant Jenny set foot on the ground, she was enfolded by—to her astonishment—the strong arms of her father.

"Jenny-girl!" he boomed, while flash guns went off on all sides. "Welcome to civilization!" Still with his arm around her, he turned toward the cluster of reporters. "Later. You'll get your story. But let's take care of Jenny first."

The family, with Hank and Bill, trooped into the kitchen. "Dad! Mom! How did you get here?" Jenny asked, staring from one to the other.

"Same way you did—by plane. Lorelei phoned us." Her father tightened his arms. "You gave us quite a fright, young lady."

There were other arms—her mother's—Lorelei's —and Lissie's and Chip's. The two children grabbed her around the knees and squeezed.

"We thought you'd never come back," piped Chip.

"It scared us an *awful lot*!" added Lissie, forgetting to be grown-up, while Honey added to the excitement with a succession of "Ah-oh, ah-oh, ah-oh," until Lorlei told Chip to cover him up, for heaven's sake.

"Jenny, why did you run away?" Chip asked, when the shawl was in place.

"I just . . ." Jenny shuddered.

"You're exhausted," her mother said, taking tight hold of her hand. "Be quiet now, all of you, and let her rest. There'll be plenty of time to talk later on." Although she spoke as crisply as always, her eyes were red, and Jenny realized with surprise that Mom —unflappable Mom—had been crying.

"Something to eat?" Lorelei asked.

"I think—ice cream. Vanilla, if you have it."

"Vanilla ice cream on its way," Lorelei replied as she reached for a bowl.

Even before she finished eating, Jenny began to nod. As if through a haze she heard her father take the names and addresses of Hank and Bill and promise them to "make it worth your while."

"Falla?" she asked with an effort. "Is he all right?"

"Right as rain," Hank assured her. "He's still in the truck, but we'll feed him and bed him down in his stall. Don't you worry about that."

So at last Jenny stumbled upstairs to bed and fell into a dreamless sleep.

The next day when she woke up, it was almost noon, and she rushed to the barn to take care of Farfalla. Back in the house, she found her breakfast ready: bacon and eggs, orange juice, toast and marmalade. Lorelei had gone to the office, but the others gathered around the table with her, leaning on their elbows, eager to hear exactly what had happened.

"Such a risky business!" Mrs. Wilson exclaimed, clucking her tongue. "To think that you slept up there two whole nights! With wild animals all around you!"

"Were you scared?" asked Chip.

"Spitless," Jenny agreed, which made Lissie giggle.

In a few moments her father folded his arms and leaned back in his chair. "Jenny, why did you go?"

he asked. "Lorelei told us Falla's former owner called, and after that you threatened to hide your horse. Did you actually think you could? Were you planning to run off?"

Jenny stopped, toast in hand. "I only wanted to figure out a plan for keeping him. Truly, I wasn't running away. I meant to come back for dinner . . ." She grinned at her heaping plate. "When I got up there, I realized I couldn't hide a horse, but I thought I'd feel better if I had a good long ride. So I tried to find a waterfall Pam had told me about, but there wasn't a trail. And when it began to rain—well—I got lost."

Her mother drew a deep breath. "I'm glad of that," she said. "You—we thought—because you sometimes . . ."

"I know!" said Jenny. "Another of my pig-headed ideas. Well, this may have *seemed* pig-headed, but for once I didn't mean it that way. It just happened."

"Seems to me you were pretty sensible, finding a place to sleep, finding water," her father said, which made Jenny laugh.

"I didn't find water! It found me! Gallons and gallons of it. Pouring on me like a river all day long!"

"Just the same, things would have been worse if you hadn't kept your head," her father insisted. "I didn't know you had it in you. You've grown up, Jenny. Learned a lot this summer."

"I was scared," she confessed. "But I thought we'd manage to get out—Falla and I." Spreading another piece of toast, slowly, with extra care, she asked the question that was banging away inside her head. "Has Mr. McEwen called again?"

"We telephoned him last evening, after you went to bed," her mother said. "More eggs?" When Jenny shook her head, she continued. "We wanted to let him know you were safe because he'd been so worried."

"Felt responsible," her father explained.

"Yes. Well, he's still at his brother's in Rock Springs, and wants to see the horse," her mother continued. "So we told him how to get in touch with the Browns in Chicago, and he wants to come here tomorrow. Will you be ready . . . ?"

"To face him? I'll be ready," Jenny said, although just thinking about it made her stomach churn. "I'd rather it would be soon, and get it over. Can't he come this afternoon?"

"No," her mother firmly said. "You need to rest."

The day was gone in a flash. Hank and Bill telephoned, to make sure she was all right.

Pam came, for Jenny to tell the whole story again. "No riding right now, for me or Falla either," she said. "For once, I've had enough!"

Lissie and Chip followed her from house to barn to house, wanting to hear all about the woods and the cave. "Bats?" Lissie asked with a shiver. "A *cougar*?"

Jenny had to repeat the story still again for Lorelei, and then, after another dreamless sleep, it was morning, and time to meet Mr. McEwen. For this,

Lorelei missed a day of work. "I'm the one the animal was dumped on," she said. "I'd better be here to explain."

Right after breakfast the doorbell rang, and when Jenny opened it, a stranger stood there, briefcase in hand. She had pictured him as big and grim, but instead he was short, stocky, and sun-browned, wearing a neat sport shirt open at the throat and a gray sweater. He looked straight at her as if sizing her up, and when he smiled, wrinkles like fans appeared beside his eyes.

When everyone was introduced and settled in the living room, Jenny perched uneasily on the edge of her chair. *Say something, somebody*, she thought and drew a grateful breath when her father began.

"Well, McEwen, did you reach the Browns?"

"I did." Mr. McEwen shook his head. "Strange people. Acted as if they thought I was trying to pin something on them." His voice was deep as Jenny remembered it from the telephone.

"And . . . ?"

"And when they finally opened up, it all fits right in. I think you've got my horse." He pulled a handful of color snapshots out of his briefcase. "I took these when he was a colt. You can see the star and the leg stripes."

As Jenny looked at the pictures, her last remnant of hope ebbed away.

The first showed a very young foal, standing beside its mother in a green field. Spindly, long-legged, it was dark brown with white stripes on the forelegs, a bit higher on the left. Just like Farfalla's.

The second was the head only, straight on, with his unmistakable star: the butterfly curves, one a little larger than the other; the narrow strip between, slightly crooked, with the same small bulge.

Other pictures showed the colt putting on weight and size, catching up to his legs. In one he was perhaps a yearling, in a field with half a dozen others of his own age.

"Well?" asked Mr. McEwen. "What do you think?"

"I—I guess—," Jenny faltered. "They look like Farfalla."

"I think so too," he replied, "although I want to see him in the flesh to make certain."

Jenny sat on the sofa and drew her chin into the collar of her sweater. *Hurry up!* she thought. *Talk fast, and get it over.*

In a moment her father spoke again. "Well, if you think so, and Jenny thinks so, it looks as if there's no doubt. But what happened? How did your colt end up in Lorelei's barn?"

Mr. McEwen leaned back in his chair and folded his arms. "I used to have a ranch over in Colorado, and for many years I raised a fine line of hunters and jumpers. My horses have run everywhere, all over the world, and some have carried royalty. Good blood lines. I like to think I know how to pick a winner."

"And you picked Farfalla?"

"M-m-m . . . say I owned him. I had a cowhand called Shiny. Nobody knew his right name, but he was a young fellow without a spear of hair on his head, so that's what he went by. Shiny wasn't over-blessed with brains, but he sure loved horseflesh. Especially this colt. Called him Montezuma and took him to be his special charge." He stopped, looking directly at Jenny, but she only shrank farther into her sweater.

"Shiny was all heart and no sense," Mr. McEwen continued. "Once when the colt got sick, he slept right in the stall. Mothered him, sort of, until we turned him out with the other youngsters. And when I decided to sell him—he was a yearling by then— Shiny was all broke up. Moped around the bunk-house, until one morning he was gone. Never did find out where. We thought it was funny, him leav-ing when he loved the colt like that."

"Anybody would love Farfalla," Jenny murmured.

"Just so. Anyhow, we didn't miss the colt until we brought in the yearlings—and he wasn't there. My hands searched the hills, but couldn't find hair nor hide of him. I had a hunch Shiny was at the bottom of it, but I never could prove a thing."

"You never found him?"

"Not until last week, and all of a sudden, there he is, big as life, on the tube. So . . . I've come to have a look."

"And Mr. Brown?" Jenny asked. "What did he say?"

Mr. McEwen grinned again. "Like I said, it all fits. At first he was mighty skittish, but when I threatened to call the police, he changed his tune. Said it was a hard thing to squeal on a friend, but if he had to, or get into a peck of trouble, why there wasn't any help for it. Then he said it was Shiny that brought him the horse. Seems they knew each other a long time back."

"But if Shiny loved Farfalla so much, why would he give him away?" asked Lorelei.

"He was on the run," Mr. McEwen replied. "Been living on the range with the horse, had a little shack away off from nowhere. Trained him, gelded him. And he appeared all of a sudden one night at the Browns's door. Said he was in trouble and had to move on, so they told him all right, they'd take care of the horse, but not for long. Next thing they knew, Shiny was hauled up on a drugs charge and put in prison for a good long term. That's why they were so sure he wouldn't come back. They didn't think the horse was worth anything, so they just left him in the barn. Made certain you knew he was there so he wouldn't starve."

"Well!" Jenny was trying to grasp all of this. "I guess it's a good thing I needed a horse for the summer. Or—"

"Or he'd have been dog food," Chip piped up in his shrillest voice. "We were going to take him to the meat place, until Jenny decided to come."

"That so?" asked Mr. McEwen, with a glance at Lorelei.

"I'm afraid it is," she admitted, turning red. "I didn't know what else to do."

"Then I thank you, Miss Jenny," the man said, the corners of his eyes gathering into wrinkles. He stood up. "I'd like to see the animal, if it's all right with you. Make sure he's the one."

"Of course," Jenny said, and they all trooped out to the barn.

There Mr. McEwen carefully compared Farfalla's markings to the pictures, looking back and forth, from one to the other. "That's him, all right. Got the same bend in the straight part, and the two halves are just that little bit lop-sided." Against her will, Jenny could see that it was undoubtedly so.

Whistling softly, Mr. McEwen felt the horse all over—flanks, shoulders, withers—and lifted the feet one by one. "He's in fine shape, Jenny. I congratulate you," he said when he was through.

"Thank you, Mr. McEwen," she replied, stroking the long, bristly face, while Falla leaned his head against her with a little sigh. At the warmth of his breath, tears filled her eyes and one of them dripped onto his fur.

"So this is the animal you almost turned into dog meat!" Mr. McEwen exclaimed, with another smile.

Lorelei made a wry face. "I'd no idea he was so young and handsome." She slipped her arm around Jenny's waist. "Jenny was the one who loved him."

"Showed mighty good taste, you did," the little man said with a smile. "Picked a winner."

"I didn't exactly pick him," Jenny said, remembering how she had fought to stay in California and ride Cinnabar. "He was just here. But I liked him—sort of—even when I thought he was old and sick." She straightened a twisted hair of his mane. "Mr. McEwen, when are you going to take him?"

"Take him!" The man stared. "You mean take him away?"

Jenny nodded.

Mr. McEwen was still staring. "Jenny . . . what kind of creature do you think I am?"

Jenny stood stock-still with her hand on Farfalla's bristly nose. Had she heard him right? Did he mean it? "I just—I was sure—Farfalla's so . . ."

Mr. McEwen shook his head. "Jenny, this is a good horse. He might turn out to be a world-beater, but it isn't likely. One in a million does that." He patted Farfalla's withers. "Like I said, he's a good horse— but that doesn't make him worth a fortune."

"You mean . . . ?" Jenny didn't have enough breath to finish the question.

"I mean I'm out of the horse business. Sold my ranch. Live in town. I've enough money and quite a bit more, and I don't want to be bothered."

"You don't *want* him?"

The fan-wrinkles were there again. "Jenny, I got along without this fellow for six years, and if it weren't for you he'd be dog meat long ago, or dead of colic."

"So . . ." Stars were going off in Jenny's head, and

she was sure that in one more second she would burst. "So Falla's *mine*? I can take him *home* with me?" She glanced at her mother and father, who were smiling too and nodding—and yes, there were tears in her mother's eyes. Mom! Crying again!

But she had to make sure about Falla. "Do you think—could I have a bill of sale?" She tried to sound business-like, although her voice was wobbly. "So I can prove Falla is really mine and nobody can take him away?"

At this Mr. McEwen began to laugh. "A bill of sale, is it? Well, Jenny, I guess we can manage that, too. For one dollar. You pay me, and I'll fix up the papers." He winked at her. "Have you got a dollar?"

"Oh, yes. Up in my room. I'll go for it right now."

"No need. This afternoon will be soon enough. I'll have your papers fixed up and bring them around then." Solemnly he held out his hand. "For now a handshake will do. Horse-traders always shake on their deals."

Jenny slipped her hand into his, feeling as if she'd been suddenly blown up like a balloon and had to hang on tight or she'd float right up to the barn ceiling and catch on a rafter. "Do you really mean it?" she asked, as they pumped their arms up and down.

"Word of honor. With all these folks for witnesses," he solemnly assured her.

Ten minutes later, Mr. McEwen was gone, driving away in his maroon automobile, while Jenny, her parents, Lorelei, and the children, stood on the porch and waved. Jenny felt as if her face were all one big smile. "He was nice, after all," she said.

"And he doesn't even want Farfalla," Lissie exclaimed. "Can we keep him?"

Lorelei shook her head. "*Jenny* can keep him. We can't take care of him, and besides, she's the one that saved his life."

"Mom? Dad?" asked Jenny, looking at her parents.

"The Dexter will house him just fine," her father said. "I draw the line at building a barn on the back lawn."

"And I can jump?"

Her mother sighed. "Even that, I suppose."

Chip, on the bottom step, was tugging at Jenny's elbow. "Don't forgt my tadpoles! You promised!"

"Okay. Tomorrow, if your mother agrees. Right now, I've got some things to do at the barn."

"We'll help you."

She started down the path with Lissie and Chip holding her hands. She was going to give Falla another bath, and this time she wouldn't let him run away. She'd use her best shampoo and walk him dry and try again to braid his mane and tail. She'd keep at it every day until she knew exactly how.

She'd have him looking just right for their next show.